Murder In Key West 2

Murder In Key West 2

MURDER AND MAYHEM IN PARADISE

Edited by Shirrel Rhoades

ABSOLUTELY AMAZING eBOOKS

ABSOLUTELY AMAZING eBOOKS

Published by Whiz Bang LLC, 926 Truman Avenue, Key West, Florida 33040, USA.

Murder In Key West 2 copyright © 2015 by Gee Whiz Entertainment LLC. Electronic compilation/ paperback edition copyright © 2015 by Whiz Bang LLC. "Vampire Slayer Murdered in Key West" copyright Michael Haskins; "The Mystery of Marina Merrick" copyright Heather Graham; "Last Chance" copyright Bill Craig; "Disturbance in the Field" copyright Roberta Isleib (Writing as Lucy Burdette); "The Walls Had Ears: Murder at 2929" copyright Ben Harrison; "Better times Than These" copyright William R. Burkett, Jr.; "The Impresario" copyright Hal Howland; "Four Fingers and the Acerbic Film Critic" copyright Shirrel Rhoades; "Hand-Fed Snapping Turtles" copyright Robert Coburn; "The Writer's End" copyright Jonathan Woods.

All rights reserved. No part of this book may be reproduced, scanned, or transmitted in any form or by any means, electronic or mechanical, including photocopying, recording, or any information storage and retrieval system, without permission in writing from the publisher. Please do not participate in or encourage piracy of copyrighted materials in violation of the author's rights. Purchase only authorized ebook editions.

This is a work of fiction. Names, characters, places, and incidents either are the product of the author's imagination or are used fictitiously, and any resemblance to actual persons, living or dead, businesses, companies, events, or locales is entirely coincidental. While the author has made every effort to provide accurate information at the time of publication, neither the publisher nor the author assumes any responsibility for errors, or for changes that occur after publication. Further, the publisher does not have any control over and does not assume any responsibility for author or third-party websites or their contents. How the ebook displays on a given reader is beyond the publisher's control.

For information contact:
Publisher@AbsolutelyAmazingEbooks.com
ISBN-13: 978-1515026211
ISBN-10: 1515026213

This second volume of *Murder In Key West* coincides with the second annual Mystery Writers Key West Fest, a conclave of famous writers, budding writers, and fans. This book is for them.

Murder In Key West 2

TABLE OF CONTENTS

Introduction
By Shirrel Rhoades

1.

Vampire Slayer Murdered in Key West
By Michael Haskins

2.

The Mystery of Marina Merrick
By Heather Graham

3.

Last Chance
By Bill Craig

4.

Disturbance in the Field
By Roberta Isleib
Writing as Lucy Burdette

5.

The Walls Had Ears:
Murder at 2929
By Ben Harrison

6.
Better Times Than These
By William R. Burkett, Jr.

7.
The Impresario
By Hal Howland

8.
Four Fingers and the Acerbic Film Critic
By Shirrel Rhoades

9.
Hand-Fed Snapping Turtles
By Robert Coburn

10.
M For Murder
By Barthélemy Banks

11.
The Writer's End
By Jonathan Woods

Introduction

Key West is an end-of-the-road town, off the beaten path. Yet four million tourists find their way each year to this Southernmost point in the continental US.

It's a fishing town. A boating town. A drinking town.

It's also a literary town.

Ernest Hemingway and Tennessee Williams lived here. So did John Ciardi, Richard Wilbur, James Leo Herlihy, and Shel Silverstein. Also Stuart Woods, Annie Dillard, and Judy Blume. Hunter S. Thompson was a frequent visitor along with Thomas McGuane and Thomas Sanchez. Jimmy Buffet is still looking for that lost shaker of salt.

But the island is most exciting as portrayed in the murder and mayhem books by such marvelous writers as Heather Graham, Michael Haskins, Bill Craig, Robert Coburn, and Lucy Burdette. They happen to be among the eleven mystery writers represented in this volume.

Contrary to the book's title, there aren't many murders here on this 2 x 4 mile island. A few stolen bicycles, petty burglaries, maybe a bar brawl or two ... but no shoot-outs with Colombian drug cartels or run-ins with dangerous Mafia thugs or face-offs with mad-dog killers.

That's the stuff of fiction, like you will find in this second volume in the *Murder In Key West* series. Here you will encounter stories by New York Times bestsellers. Shamus nominees. Spinetingler winners. Lorian

i

Hemingway Short Story Competition winners. Amazon bestsellers. AP award-winners. Agatha, Anthony, and Macavity short-listers.

These writers are masters of imagination, creating might-have-been tales of mystery and suspense. Perfect beach reading. Or rainy day reading. Or up-after-midnight reading.

I know you will enjoy them as much as I did.

- Shirrel Rhoades
Key West

1.
VAMPIRE SLAYER MURDERED IN KEY WEST

Michael Haskins

That was the double-decked, 48-point headline of the daily Key West Citizen and probably a few other newspapers in South Florida the following day. It was a little misleading but it did its job because stories on vampires and murders sell newspapers.

When Monroe County Sheriff's Deputy Harry Sawyer rocked my sailboat, *Fenian Bastard*, and called my name, it was four in the morning and I didn't know about the murder. When you live on a boat and someone is trying to wake you that early it usually means you're sinking so you react fast; good news doesn't come knocking at four A.M.

I was outside in seconds. "What?" I yelled. It took a minute in the dark to realize it was Harry because he was out of uniform.

"Mick, you didn't answer the phone," he said as if that explained why he was there. "The sheriff wants you on Stock Island."

Stock Island is the first island across the bridge when leaving Key West. Part of it is city property but the largest section belongs to the county.

"Me?" I yawned and went below. The good news was my sailboat wasn't sinking.

Harry followed. "Yeah, he woke me at home and told me to bring you to the old mansion at the end of Fifth Street." He stood in the hatchway. "Right away."

"Why?" I fumbled into a pair of cargo shorts, put on yesterday's T-shirt and grabbed my sun-faded Boston Red Sox cap that accented my shaggy red hair and beard.

"He hung up before saying," Harry grinned. "But it sounded urgent."

Bob Pearlman is the county sheriff. We have met socially and I found it curious he'd call me out at this hour. My experiences have shown that law enforcement and journalists are as compatible as spaghetti sauce and a white shirt.

"No ideas Harry?" I walked up the dock with him.

"It's my day off, Mick, so I'm not even sure what they're working on," he said. "Ride with me, maybe something will come over the radio."

~~~

"Do you know her?" Sheriff Pearlman asked as we stood in the living room of the crumbling mansion.

I looked down at the naked body but my eyes focused on the crude wooden stake driven into the victim's chest. It was an attention grabber.

"Do you?" he asked again, agitated.

I looked at the woman's ashen face. I saw her fogged brown eyes, heavily outlined in black, and the fear frozen in her final expression; messy shoulder length hair, black as crow's feathers, spread out on the floor alongside her head and lips that were exaggerated by smudged red gloss. Someone had carefully crossed her arms below the wooden stake. One piercing accented the left side of her nose and multiple studs highlighted her earlobes. An open gash exposed raw flesh on her abdomen. She didn't remind me of anyone I knew.

"No," I finally answered. "Should I?"

"She's one of yours," Sheriff Pearlman said seriously.

"Mine?" I didn't know what he meant; did he think I killed her?

"It's Tracy Cox, the journalist," he explained coldly.

My name is Liam Murphy but I picked up the moniker Mad Mick Murphy in college because of crazy pranks I got involved in and my Irish heritage. I'm a journalist and live on my sailboat in Key West, Florida.

Knowing we're both journalists, the sheriff believed Tracy and I traveled in the same circles. We didn't. She wrote long investigative pieces that were often published as books; I wrote when weekly newsmagazines or a Miami news services called me, otherwise I sailed.

The Tracy Cox I knew of was not into the Gothic look, but the pile of black clothing next to the body hinted otherwise about the victim, only the wooden stake wasn't an accessory.

"Where'd the blood go?" I asked, curious about the lack of it.

"Killed somewhere else and then moved here," the sheriff said matter-of-factly. "There's no such thing as vampires, if that's what you're thinking, though someone went to a lot of work to make it look otherwise," he muttered harshly and frowned at me.

I looked down again and went right to the stake, moved to her face and stared.

"Tracy has dirty blonde hair," I said. "I met her a long time ago at an award's dinner. This isn't her."

The Sheriff smirked. "It's her. I met her a month ago in Miami and she had the black hair and piercings. The FBI called us rural sheriffs together and she was the guest."

"Guest for what?" He had piqued my curiosity.

The sheriff led me into the next room as crime scene people began their work.

"They wanted us yokels to be aware of a theft ring that could be moving to the countryside, maybe the Keys," he said bitterly. "Tracy Cox told the story. She informed the FBI about it just before publishing her newspaper series and then the group went underground. She thought Florida was ripe for what they did."

The room might have been the mansion's library once, but the shelves were empty and dusty and the gray light of dawn accentuated the cracked, dirty windows.

"Theft of what?" I yawned and wished I were back in bed.

"Body parts," he said casually.

"Body parts?" I was no longer sleepy.

"Got your attention, did I?" he said coarsely.

"Yeah." And he told me the sordid story.

~~~

After-hour Gothic clubs in the big cities, New York, Miami, Los Angeles, and the like, had cliques of vampire wannabes and some of them were true believers in the messages that TV programs and cult movies profited from. The clubs didn't advertise, or have signs outside, they didn't need to, word-of-mouth filled them, especially on weekends.

For the past year, bodies of young men and women were showing up in these cities, minus a kidney, liver, or heart and even eyes. Attending Gothic clubs and being young were two items that connected the victims. Missing body parts was another.

Tracy Cox went undercover and began a series about New York clubs where vampire devotees with surgically implanted dental fangs role-played and actually drank each other's blood. And, she discovered a mesmerizing older vampire disciple. After her story appeared in the paper the club closed, the disciple vanished, and one tabloid called her the vampire slayer. The title stuck.

"What do you want from me?" I looked back into the room and Tracy's body was covered with a tarp, waiting on the medical examiner.

"People talk to you," the sheriff said slowly, "see what you hear about a Gothic club starting up. I don't want to find kids stuck in the mangroves missing body parts."

~~~

I only know one Gothic kid and it was a presumption on my part because when I saw him at the marina he always dressed in black, had a pale complexion, piercings and if I caught him in daylight it was as we passed coming and going in the early morning. He had changed in the last few months, losing most piercings, and actually hung around the dock some afternoons.

"Alex," I called out his name when I spotted him in the shade of his houseboat's overhang. "What are you reading?"

"A book," he smiled and gulped from his coffee cup.

"You got a minute?"

"Sure, come aboard." He closed the book.

"You going to school?" I saw a textbook, as I sat down.

"City College," he said. "Time to get educated."

You don't ask personal questions to boat people. You know what they want you to know, so I knew little about Alex. He looked young, possibly not even twenty-one. He bought the houseboat two years ago and moved in. He was quiet and kept to himself. On occasion, he showed up at one of our infamous dock parties where the food was homemade and liquor flowed for hours. Sometimes he drank and ate, sometimes he shared a joint and other times he walked on without stopping.

"You choose a major?" I tried to sound interested.

"Maybe biology," he lied.

I have a built-in BS detector and returned his smile without saying anything.

"If I tell you the truth you won't laugh." He leaned toward me. "Or tell anyone else on the dock."

"If it's funny, I'm gonna laugh," I said. "But whatever it is, it's between us."

"Police science," he muttered and sat straight up. "I signed up for the police academy and filled out the papers to be a city cop."

"That's great," I said.

"What if nobody on the dock will talk to me when they see the uniform," he frowned. He was young enough to care what others thought.

"Or everyone will feel safer knowing a cop lives at the marina," I said.

He smiled his reply.

"I'm wondering if you can help me." I asked after an uneasy moment of silence.

"With what?" He sat back to be more comfortable or distance himself from my request, I am not sure which.

"Is there a Goth club in town?" I tried to say without too much of a silly grin.

"There's a new hangout on the water," he said suspiciously. "Why?"

"I'd like you to go there with me."

He must of though it was funny because he burst out laughing.

"Yeah," he tried to say as he gulped air, "you'd fit right in, just like I would at the yacht club."

He had a point and when he stopped laughing I told him, in a round about way, about the murder of Tracy Cox and how it was thought to be related to her series on Gothic clubs.

"I read a few of her stories online," he said more in

control now that he had stopped laughing. "Did you know her?"

"Yeah," I lied and was glad he didn't have his own BS detector. "I want to look into what happened and maybe finish her series."

"Mick, with red hair, a beard and a tan a tourist would kill for," he hesitated, probably wondering if saying the word kill was in bad taste. When I didn't reply he went on. "You'd draw more attention to yourself than a centerfold shoot on Duval Street."

"Hadn't thought of that," I admitted realizing he was also young enough to look at Playboy and not read the articles. "Where is this place?"

He got us coffee and told me about an old yacht that moved off Christmas Tree Island in Key West Harbor about two months ago and hosted Gothic themed parties.

"After midnight there's a shuttle boat that picks you up at the Simonton Street Pier," he said. "I've gone a couple of times, but, like I said, I'm moving in another direction now."

"How does the boat know who to pick up?'

He gave me a quizzical look and shook his head. "It wouldn't pick you up, that's for sure. If you look like you belong, you can get in the boat."

"And you look the part?"

"A hell of a lot more than you do."

"Do you know who owns the yacht?"

"An older guy, older than you." He finished his coffee. "I don't mean anything negative, it's just that everyone there is young, high school or college age. But this guy is creepy, like he believes he's Dracula."

"What do you mean?" He had my full attention.

"He's whiter than me, has fangs and speaks with a Spanish accent," he said. "I dated an English girl back home that wasn't that pale. He makes his rounds of the party a few times and then disappears below deck. Maybe he keeps his coffin there," he laughed.

"Who runs the party then?"

"Two hot babes," Alex smiled. "There's a couple of dudes off in the shadows and I think they're security, but I don't know for sure."

"I need to get on board and snoop around." I ran my fingers across my beard. "Maybe dye my hair."

"And bleach your skin, look like Michael Jackson," he shook his head and laughed. "Look, if it's that important to you, I can put a few studs back in my ears and do your snooping."

I guess he really did want to be a cop. Goth to cop, go figure.

"Tell me what you're looking for and I'll go tonight." He was getting excited.

I didn't like sending someone to do my legwork, but he had a point about me standing out. There was no way I would fit into the Gothic scene. My presence could make them suspicious and possibly they'd disappear again. Or, maybe they had other ways of dealing with snooping journalists.

~~~

I tried to get a look at the yacht Alex mentioned from the Glass Bottom Boat dock at the end of Duval Street. The Sunset Pier at the Ocean Key Resort blocked my view, but I did see the yacht's outline. I cut through the resort and found a good viewing spot at Mallory Square.

My guess about the anchored yacht was it had to be 100-foot long, wooden hull and was once beautiful; a large, open aft deck, and inside there was sure to be a roomy salon with staterooms below, a galley and crews quarters, too; an engine room in the lower aft section, an enclosed bridge above the salon.

Today, the yacht fit in with the background of

Christmas Tree Island and its dissolute pine trees and landscape. Across the channel, Sunset Key and its million dollar homes sparkled in comparison. Once the old ship might have belonged with expensive island homes, but now it bobbed in Key West Harbor while Jet Ski riders zipped past, as if it was a forgotten stepchild. The yacht anchored far enough offshore to keep it from city jurisdiction.

"The gates of hell," came from a voice behind me. I turned to see Padre Thomas Collins.

Padre Thomas is an Irish-born Jesuit missionary that walked away from his mission in Guatemala when the angels he sees and talks to told him to. Soon afterward, the rightwing junta's soldiers massacred most of the villagers and Padre Thomas still suffers from survivor's guilt all these years later. He's medium height, thin as a rail, and slowly losing his hair. He gets around town on an old bicycle and chain-smokes cigarettes. He's sixty if he's a day. Or maybe guilt has aged him.

"Padre Thomas," I greeted him and waited for his explanation.

"I thought I'd find you here," he wheezed and lit a new cigarette. "What are you going to do?"

It is scary how he often knows what I'm doing before I do. "About what?" I said without conviction.

Padre Thomas pointed to the yacht.

"Beautiful old boat," I smiled. "Why'd you call it the gates of hell?" I turned away and looked back at the water.

"Because the devil lives there," he sighed callously. He wasn't joking.

"Lucifer or one of his fallen angels?" I tried not to laugh.

Padre Thomas moved up next to me. "Evil resides on that boat," he whimpered.

I looked at the old yacht and my curiosity wondered

about its history. Who had sailed on her, partied, laughed and was happy? When had the gaiety of past lives turned into the gates of hell? And, if it leads to hell, why hadn't the wooden boat burst into flames?

I didn't say what I was thinking. Instead, I put my arm around his bony shoulders and turned him away. "People are looking into it, Padre," I said. "People that can do something about it, unlike you and me."

We headed toward the Hog's Breath Saloon for happy hour.

"It's in your hands, Mick," he said without a trace of a smile. "And time is running out."

~~~

My phone rang at five A.M. the next morning.

"Meet me at Harpoon's in a half hour," Alex said when I answered.

"Alex? What time is it?" I muttered, half awake.

"The time vampires go back into their coffins," he laughed. "Bring some paper and pencils too. Half an hour, Mick." He hung up.

I dressed hurriedly, again, and drove my old white Jeep to Harpoon Harry's. At the early hour I didn't have a problem parking, but it irked me to put so many quarters into the meter.

Ron, the owner, smiled as I came in. Alex sat at a table in the back.

"*Con leche*, Ron," I said as I passed and knew he'd make the Cuban *café con leche* I drink. It's espresso with steamed milk and too much sugar. I am addicted to it.

Alex looked wide-awake and sipped regular coffee.

"You ain't gonna believe this," Alex said with a grin. "Did you bring the paper and pencils?"

I put the rolled up paper and two mechanical pencils on the table.

We ordered breakfast and while we waited Alex began

drawing.

"Things are getting weird out there," he said. The studs were still in his ear.

"How?" I sipped my *con leche.*

"The babes I told you about," he looked up at me and smiled. "They wanted to suck my blood. I saw them sucking on a guy's neck, a girl's arm, and another girl's neck, more than once." He finished one sheet and began on another. "Also, get this, they were asking everyone onboard if they'd donate blood for *The Master*. Yeah, that's what they called the old guy, *The Master*."

"Donate blood?" I was waking up quickly. "How?"

"Just like in the doctor's office, Mick." He looked up. "You know, needle in the arm and a big tube to fill."

"Did they have any takers?"

Our breakfast came and Alex moved his drawings aside and we ate.

"More than I thought they'd get," he said with a mouthful of egg and toast. "If you give, you get to go below."

"For what? What's the attraction down below?"

"Hell if I know, I ain't givin' blood, even though the babes are hot," he smiled and stuffed the remaining egg into his mouth. "I stay away from anything that involves a needle, especially if it's used more than once."

He slid the first sheet of paper to me, it was the floor plan of the yacht, and continued to work on a second sheet.

"There's a go-fast boat on the starboard side." He kept drawing and didn't look up. "You can't see it from land. The measurements on that are a guess, I paced off the lengths," he said about the footage figures on the paper I held. "You ain't gonna believe this," he said again and handed the second drawing to me.

Alex had drawn a headshot of *The Master*, sardonic

11

smile showing fangs, and he looked a lot like Hollywood's image of Dracula.

~~~

I stood with Sheriff Pearlman and Key West Police Chief Richard Dowley at the railing on the deck of the Sunset Tiki Bar, sweating in the bright sun, and we had a good view of Christmas Tree Island and the yacht. They held copies of Alex's two drawings.

The yacht was anchored far enough offshore to be in county waters, so the city police could do nothing. The sheriff didn't have the manpower to patrol the waters surrounding the Florida Keys, he depended on the state marine patrol to do that and the Coast Guard.

They talked about the need for warrants and the evidence necessary to get a warrant. Richard could have the nightshift patrol the parking lot of the Simonton Pier to see who went there. Chances were good that someone would show up with an outstanding warrant, eventually, and then they would have a person to question about the yacht. Maybe even get enough for a warrant on suspicion of drug use or underage drinking. Maybe.

We talked about having Capt. Fitton of the Coast Guard look in to the yacht's history, see if it was certified, had a legal holding tank and safety equipment; the Coast Guard could board her to check on these things. We tossed around a lot of options.

The sheriff thanked me for what I had done and promised to keep me appraised on his investigation. I didn't believe him, but he didn't seem bothered by that. Richard knew me better than Sheriff Pearlman did. Richard turned for a second time as he and the sheriff left the Tiki Bar, and his puckered brow told me he was concerned. I should have been too.

As a journalist, I have rules to go by. Get the story right and present it honestly. The rule for getting the story is simple: anything goes. I don't have the restrictions law enforcement does, but I don't have their back up either, I was alone.

After breakfast with Alex, I had this nagging question about *The Master's* Spanish accent. I read Tracy's articles online that night and she speculated the disciple was Puerto Rican. In New York that made sense, but in South Florida, the accent would make him Cuban.

I had a hunch and old-time journalists did legwork because of their hunches. What I needed to find out wasn't in recorded files, so it wouldn't show up on Google.

As I left the Tiki Bar, I called a waterfront character I was acquainted with and offered to buy him a drink. He'd given me background material for stories before, but this time I was hoping for more.

~~~

Bob Pierce had to be in his late fifties. He was born and raised in the Keys and worked his way through college with the proceeds he made smuggling square grouper and powerboat racing. He stayed below the radar and that kept him out of jail, even when the Feds made the local Bubba Bust in the '80s for drug smuggling.

"They are the last remnants of old Key West," Bob drawled as he looked at the shrimp boat fleet from the seawall of Safe Harbor on Stock Island.

"So I hear," I agreed about the shrimp boats.

"The older I get the less I like change," he sighed.

We were on our second bottle of beer and left the bar for the privacy of the seawall.

"I've got a hunch about something and I thought maybe you'd be the guy to check with," I said and swallowed beer.

Bob looked suspiciously at me and smiled, but said nothing.

I unfolded the portrait Alex had done and handed it to

him. His smile grew.

"Dracula?" He almost laughed.

"Forget the fangs," I finished my beer. "Look familiar?"

"Wouldn't know him from Adam." He handed me back the drawing. "Who is he?"

"That's what I want to know."

"You wearing a wire?" He trusted no one; it was a way of life for him.

"You know better."

"That's not a no." He finished his beer and walked to the bar. He returned with two beers, our third so far. "Yes or no." He held the beer out to me.

"No," I said and took the bottle. "This is personal. Could lead to a story."

"Let me tell you a story." He took a long gulp from the bottle. "There's this captain who brings in refugees from Cuba. First he did it because a girl he knew wanted her family here, then because someone offered him money for a relative and soon it was a lot of money for a lot of relatives."

Bob leaned against a palm tree and drank. This was his story, so I let him tell it his way, but we both knew he was the captain.

"One day he was approached by someone who offered him a lot of money," he smiled. "Notice how it always involves lots of money?"

"I noticed."

"There was one rule, the captain could only bring back his people, no extra cargo. The money was good, so the captain said okay. He showed up at Marina Hemingway on a certain day, went to a certain bar . . ."

"And meet a certain somebody," I cut him off. "We getting to the point?"

"If you're in a hurry, Mick, you should've come

yesterday and we'd be done by now," he grinned. "Can I go on?"

I nodded.

"Anyway, since you're buying I'll cut to the chase," he finished his beer. "The people were at the bar like he was told they would be, they met and went to the marina with the captain, passed through security and were in Summerland Key a few hours later. You know how hard it is for a Cuban with a suitcase to get into Marina Hemingway, not to mention on a boat?"

"Impossible, I would've said."

"Me too." He walked to bar and came back with our fourth beer. "Anyway, at Summerland Key this captain is met by someone in a van, gets paid the second half of the fee and all is well with the world as he heads back to Key West."

"A good story, but what does it have to do with him?" I shook the folded paper.

"This captain made the trip a few more times for the person and it was always the same. Then, one day, this person offers him the full-boat-load fee to pick up one passenger," he leaned back against the palm tree again. "Lots of money for very little work."

"And?"

"Well, if Dracula's face was a little thinner with a mustache instead of fangs, that could be him in your drawing," he said without losing his smile.

"How many years ago?"

"Two, maybe a little more."

"What did the captain think of all this?"

"Now you want the whole story," he laughed. "The captain is fluent in Spanish but the Cubans don't know that, so they talk freely among themselves. Basically, the person has brought them over, paid their fees, and in return they've agreed to give him a kidney when he can match them as a donor. Gotta be a doctor."

Hunches sometimes pay off, I thought to myself.

"Any recent trips?" I said.

"Not for a year." He finished the beer. "Not for the doctor, anyway."

"Does the captain know how to get in touch with the doctor?" I was excited because I just about had the bastard.

"No name," he said. "But this captain has a pornographic memory."

"Photographic," I correct him.

"No," he grinned and tore the label off the bottle. "Pornographic, everything is dirty to him," he laughed. "He took the plate number of the van, call it curiosity or self-preservation, because the person knew him, but the captain didn't know squat about the person. Turns out the van is registered to a small hospital in the middle of the state."

"You gonna make me beg?"

"No, I'm going to make you buy lunch." He turned and walked toward the bar.

I got what I needed from Bob during lunch, which wasn't another beer, the hospital's name, address and phone number. I hadn't felt this excited about a story in a long time. I could use Google to find out more, including the names of hospital staff. Somehow, somewhere the hospital was connected to the Gothic yacht, I knew it, I just had to find the connection.

~~~

I should have called Richard or Sheriff Pearlman, but I didn't. I went back to *Fenian Bastard*, Googled the hospital and printed out pages of information on it, including a list of its medical staff. Focusing on the medical staff was a long shot, but so was going to see Bob, and I was parlaying my hunches. In the big city you would've called the small hospital a clinic, but not in the Everglades.

Padre Thomas found me eating a fish sandwich for dinner at Schooner Wharf Bar. I was alone in the bar's mezzanine poolroom going over the information about the hospital, when he walked in.

"Time is running out, Mick," he said as greeting.

"Time for what, Padre?"

"To stop the evil." He sat down and lit a cigarette. "To beat the devil."

"It's a slow process," I said and shook the paperwork at him. "But it is moving forward."

"Are those Tracy's notes?" He exhaled smoke through his nose.

"No," I said. "How would I get Tracy's notes?"

"I thought you went to her house."

His words surprised me. "You know where she stayed?"

"Yes." He stubbed out the cigarette. "I contacted her when she first arrived."

The day was full of surprises and all of them good.

"How . . ." I didn't finish because his look told me I knew how, even if I didn't want to believe it. I didn't like to admit belief in his angels, but sometimes there was no other explanation. "Is it in Old Town?"

"A couple of blocks down by the cemetery." He lit another cigarette.

"She was watching the cemetery?" I left money for my dinner under the ashtray.

"No," he groaned. "She wasn't interested in the dead, she cared about the living. You don't believe in vampires, do you?"

We walked to my Jeep. "I believe in everything, Padre," I said. "Sometimes, even your angels."

~~~

Tracy's rental house was on Angela Street, across from the Key West Cemetery, as Padre Thomas said. It was an old two-bedroom, one bath, cigar cottage like so many others on the island that were constructed by ship builders for cigar factory rollers at the turn of the twentieth-century. Some have withstood the tropical sun, hurricanes and termites for more than one hundred years.

I used a credit card to slip the front door lock. Most people in the neighborhood didn't bother with modern door locks.

The living room furniture looked as old as the house. The second bedroom was Tracy's office and thick wooden planks served as her desk. Her laptop was still on and the screensaver flashed a selection of photos, some of Tracy smiling without a stake in her chest, and others of children that must have been her nieces and nephews.

"What are we looking for?" Padre Thomas asked from the doorway.

I sat at the table and hit the shift button. The screen came to life but I was disappointed because it held only a few file folders. I opened the folder that was labeled vampire, but it was her series from New York.

"We've gotta find her USB storage disk." I looked around the table, other than reference books it was clean.

"Would she have had it with her? In a purse?" Padre Thomas stayed in the doorway.

"I don't know, but she'd have a backup or two," I said because I always kept backups, especially when I was away from home. "Somewhere in the house. If she was being cautious, she hid it."

The only thing in the office closet was an opened carton of computer paper.

The bedroom was as sparse as the living room. An unmade bed, a small nightstand and bureau. I went through everything as thoroughly as I could but found no disk. Padre Thomas searched the tiny kitchen and I heard him moving pots and pans around.

I found nothing under the sofa pillows in the living room. A stack of paperback books, a few magazines, and a beer can cigarette lighter were on the coffee table. I checked each book, thinking she might have hollowed out one and hid items in it. I was wrong.

Padre Thomas picked up the lighter and snapped it continuously to light his cigarette. It didn't ignite.

"Who keeps a lighter that doesn't work," he grumbled and shook it. "It must need lighter fluid." He opened it. "It's dry," he said. "No wonder it won't light." He lit his cigarette with a match.

I took the lighter, pulled the stuffing out of the bottom, and found her small USB storage disk hidden inside. "Got it," I said and almost laughed.

"What do you think is on it?" Padre Thomas asked and stubbed out his cigarette.

"Let's find out." We went to her office and used the laptop.

Tracy had been the ultimate note taker. All pages were dated. Some were no more than a thought, while others were a page or two. Names, dates, contact information, the wherefore and the whys of the information. The most helpful were her personal thoughts on the information or who gave it to her. I was impressed.

I had the link she was looking for, the hospital. She had gone undercover to find out who pulled *The Master's* strings. She wanted to know what he did with the body parts, who they went to and why. She considered it was a cannibalistic ritual, but had her doubts.

"Padre, what do you think of all this?" I asked when I closed down the laptop and put the disk in my pocket.

"She was closing in on the Devil, Mick," he hissed and lit a cigarette. "He killed her."

"It's more than one man, Padre, it's a whole group of them," I said and stood. "I don't think it's cannibalism, there's no money in that."

"That leaves what?" he asked as we left the house.

"There's money to be made in supplying body parts, if you can find a donor that is a good match to the recipient." It wasn't my idea Tracy had considered it too.

~~~

I took Padre Thomas home.

On the boat, I went through the files on Tracy's disk again and printed out a few that interested me, piqued my interest. I lit a cigar and went out on deck to read them. I reread them after my cigar was gone, but my conclusion remained the same. It was a lot of guesswork on my part, on Tracy's too, but reading between the lines of what she'd written, adding my own hunches to her's, it was bad no matter how I looked at it.

Her conclusions were logical, even if unproved. The cops would say there wasn't enough evidence for a warrant. No warrant, no search. I didn't need a warrant, I needed a way onto the yacht so I could turn speculation into fact.

"What are you doing up at the witching hour?" Alex asked from the dock.

I hadn't been paying attention to anything going on around me. "Trying to make sense out of someone's note," I said. "What are you doing?"

"I was downtown listening to Clint Bullard. I walked, so it took a while," he said explaining the late hour. "Anything happening on the other thing?"

"Not officially," I told him. "But I'm working on something."

"Need help?" There was a slight hint of excitement in his question.

He came onboard. I told him about my need to get

onto the yacht and asked if he could think of a way. I told him I needed to get below, unseen.

"There's an aft hatch to the engine room," he said. "There has to be an entrance from the engine room to the lower section, wouldn't you think?"

"Yeah," I mused. "There has to be more than one way in and out."

"The hatch is behind storage lockers," he said. "I noticed it when I was pacing off the deck. I didn't see a lock on it, but I wasn't really looking for one. It could be locked from below."

"How well is it lit and what goes on out there?"

"Most of the light comes from the salon windows, but there is an anchor light," he said. "I don't think they encourage anyone to be outside."

"That's a good thing," I smiled.

A white light at the aft section of any anchored boat is a maritime safety requirement and without one authorities can board and ticket you. The yacht was in compliance.

~~~

My boarding plan was simple. The difficult part would begin when I got on deck. Alex was excited about helping, but I didn't share that excitement though I needed him in place in case things went wrong. A late-night call to my friend Burt found him downtown and willing to help with the skiff.

Alex took the shuttle boat at Simonton Pier and knew to signal when it was safe for me to board.

It went like clockwork. At one-thirty, the sky was cloudy and the Gulf side of the yacht was dark. Alex signaled, a wave of his arms, and Burt dropped me off. I brought my Glock, a small laser flashlight and a pry bar for the engine room hatch. I dressed all in black, T-shirt, jeans, tennis shoes and watch cap that I pulled over my red hair. I quietly climbed the ladder from the yacht's tethered go-fast to the deck.

Alex smoked a cigarette on the aft deck and I heard him talking loudly to someone. I hugged the salon's outside wall and waited for Alex and his friend to go inside. I crawled to the storage lockers and sat on the deck next to the engine room hatch. The anchor light shined from a short pole and gave enough illumination for me to work. The hatch was locked from inside, just like the hatches on *Fenian Bastard*. Music escaped the salon and thankfully it was punk rock so it was more noise than comfortable listening music. Prying the hatch loose was easy because of its age, but it did make a loud popping sound as the two screw locks below gave way. Of course, at that hour the sound carried.

I waited to see if anyone would investigate the noise. They didn't. I raised the hatch, dropped the pry bar overboard and climbed below. I needed the flashlight to find my way through the dark engine room. A door led to the yacht's bright, carpeted hallway and staterooms.

There were two doors on either side of the hallway and one at the end. Noise of people gathered in the salon and the recorded music could be heard by the stairway to the salon but it was muted.

I wasn't sure what I was looking for but knew I'd recognize it when I found it. Searching for the unknown is like that. There wouldn't be a problem getting a search warrant once I delivered the proof. Of course, I didn't know the proof of what. Tracy had suspicions and so did I. We came up with our suspicions from two different directions; she had what I was missing and I had what she needed, so something was here.

I tried the door closest to the engine room, on the right. It was a small stateroom with double berths. I tried the door across the hall. It was dark inside. I searched the wall for a switch and turned the lights on.

And found all the evidence the police would need.

In the middle of the large room, there was a gurney with an unconscious young man covered to his shoulders by a sheet. I pulled my Glock and closed the door. This had been two staterooms but they were guttered to make one large hospital-styled room, with metal storage cabinets, ceiling lights, IV stands and portable trays. The kid was hooked up to a heart monitor that quietly beeped and an IV. At least he was still alive.

He looked like he was sleeping, but I guessed it was IV induced. His blood pressure was 120 over 80 and his heart rate was 65. I thought the numbers were good and removed the IV needle. He didn't yelp when the tape pulled at the hair on his arm. The heart monitor caused a problem because an alarm would be set off if the heartbeat stopped. If someone, somewhere was monitoring it, things would go to hell very quickly. I left it alone for the time being.

The thought made me nervous and I searched the ceiling and walls for possible security cameras, but found none.

I slapped his face. He didn't wake or show he even felt it. His black clothing lay neatly folded on a chair. There was no wallet in his pants. A few dollars and some change was all. I turned on the bathroom light and shut off the overhead light so the glow wouldn't show under the door.

When Richard answered my call, I knew I'd awakened him. It was after two A.M. and he was home sleeping. I told him where I was and what I had. He was angry and then he was concerned because he couldn't send city cops. He hung up after assuring me he was calling Sheriff Pearlman and Capt. Fitton at the Coast Guard right away.

I cracked the door and checked the hallway. Nothing. I went back and slapped the boy again, twice. He didn't even flinch. I couldn't carry him up through the hatch and overboard. He was too big. I could hide him in the engine room and that would keep him away from *The Master* and his two goons, briefly.

The center door to the bow area was locked. The other door was unlocked and the room was dark. Light from the hallway illuminated a stateroom with a single bed, a TV and small stereo. The main suite, I guessed and closed the door.

I figured to grab the kid's clothes and carry him fireman style to the engine room, hide him there in the dark and sneak on deck to wait for the Coast Guard. I went into the room and turned on the lights.

"And who are you?"

The Master, or Dracula, or whomever he was he was supposed to be, stood next to the gurney and startled me. Tall, thin, dressed totally in black and when he spoke I saw his fangs. Unbelievable.

The Glock was in my hand. I did it automatically, without thinking. I had him. I looked around for something to tie him up with.

"You're here to save him?" He pointed to the unconscious boy and laughed quietly. It was not a funny laugh.

"Move away from the boy." I pointed the gun at him, but he didn't seem to notice or care, if he did. "Now."

He backed up two steps and smiled, his play-actor fangs glittering in his mouth.

"How do you expect to get him out?" he said harshly. "My men upstairs will stop you. All those fools upstairs will help them, you cannot escape."

"The three of us can stay here and wait for the Coast Guard." I locked the door. "Then I don't have to do anything but turn you over."

"They are coming?"

"Oh yeah, I've called."

"That's too bad," he grinned and stared with hard eyes toward me. "Now so many will die, including the boy and you."

"Just stay still and no one has to die," I said, thinking I was in charge because I had the gun.

"Do you think *you* can kill me?" he laughed contemptuously. "Take this body, it can't serve me any longer." He walked around the gurney toward me. "Smell that?"

"I don't smell anything. Stay still," I warned him. "I *will* shoot."

"No doubt," he smirked. "You and the others will burn to death."

He kept coming. I shot past him as a warning, but he kept coming.

"You'll need to shoot better than that," he snorted and showed his fangs.

I shot him in the heart twice. He smiled.

"I will see you soon," he said clearly and then fell to the floor, dead.

I opened the door to see if anyone was coming and I smelled the smoke and heard the panic cries from the salon. I pulled the heart monitor wrap off kid's arm, lifted him over my shoulder and rushed upstairs, the Glock in my hand. If the goons were there I would shoot them too. Kids were coming down the stairs and I forced some of them back with the gun.

"They've locked us in, Mick," Alex said as he headed toward the stairway. "I figured you were below." His voice wasn't panicked. "Burt out there?"

"Yeah and the Coast Guard's on its way," I told him. The kid was getting heavy. "Where are his people?"

"Don't know," he said as young men and women trampled over each other and banged on the glass doors looking for escape. "Figure they did this?"

I grabbed a kid, about six foot and stopped him. "Look for a fire extinguisher," I yelled.

He pushed away and went to the door. Flames jumped on the aft deck and smoke began to come into the salon from the bow section.

"Take him," I said to Alex and gave him the unconscious boy.

Alex carried him as I did. I pushed my way to the doors, shot at the glass and it shattered offering an escape from the salon. Heat forced its way in and pushed us back.

"Get out," I yelled and shot into the air. "Overboard, quickly." I pushed people through the opening.

Flames swiftly spread along the deck as the kids ran. Alex came up and looked at the flames that almost engulfed the whole aft.

"Burt's gotta be out there, run and jump," I told him.

"When you do," he said.

"Save him." I slapped the kid on Alex's shoulder. "I'll be right behind you."

Alex looked at me and I could see his doubt, but he pulled the sheet over the kid's head and ran toward the right side of the boat and through the flames. I willed the deck to hold him and looked back inside.

Smoke filled the salon and I heard frightened kids crying for help, but couldn't see them. Heat came in with a boiling force that kept the thick smoke building up inside. I was on my knees listening to those calling out. My eyes watered and it was difficult to breathe. Reluctantly, I crawled away from the smoky salon and toward the flames, knowing the safety of water was close.

The yacht was no longer the gates to hell, it was hell.

My whole body was heated to where I wanted to cry out and tear away my clothing. I stood in the last small spot on the deck that wasn't burning and found myself surrounded by an inferno. Flames rushed across the top deck and the bridge was nothing but a sparkling blaze. The storage lockers were an unseen hazard in front of me, hidden behind the dancing flames. I had either side to run to but in the crackling sound of the flames, I heard sections of deck give away too. I took short breaths because there was no air to draw from, only burning heat. I couldn't wait, I ran left through the fire, the way I'd come in, and stumbled over the side rail and knew I'd singed my beard as I tumbled into the water trying not to hear the cries from the salon.

"Took you long enough," Burt yelled as he and Alex pulled me onto the skiff that was already overloaded with frightened kids.

The fire department's boat poured water on the smoldering yacht and other boats slowly cruised the surrounding water looking for survivors.

~~~

A few days later I stood smoking a cigar on the boardwalk outside Schooner Wharf and looked toward Christmas Tree Island. The smoldering shell of the yacht had been towed to the Coast Guard base. Chief Richard Dowley and Padre Thomas were with me. Six kids had died in the salon and two drowned. Counting *The Master*, nine died because of the fire. Of course, *The Master* was dead before the fire.

"No idea who he was," Richard said slowly. "No return on the finger prints. But we got records off his computer. The FBI is investigating the Everglades clinic."

"What about the two goons and the babes?" I swallowed beer from the bottle I held and wondered if the sheriff would keep me in the loop, like he promised. "Did they start the fire and leave?"

"We're not sure, but the go-fast was gone when the fire department arrived," he sighed. "We assume they got away in the boat because all the bodies have been identified, they were students. He didn't start it because he was with you, then his people did. Why wouldn't they wait for him?"

"What's on the computer?" I finished the beer and didn't tell Richard *The Master* seemed to know I was going to kill him. It was too early in the day for the beer and cigar, but I enjoyed them anyway.

"Nothing we could have used against him," Richard laughed at the irony. "He had no reason to panic."

"What was on it?" I asked again. There had to be something if the FBI was interested in the clinic.

"He was using the kid's blood to check their compatibility for body part donations, filing away their blood types and other information for later," Richard said seriously. He held an empty coffee cup. "Nothing illegal about it. You can donate your kidney."

"It was more than that," I said.

"I believe you, but we can't prove it, yet."

"What about the boy I found?"

"He remembers nothing. He was upstairs with your babes and then he woke up naked in the water," Richard grunted. "He's gone home."

I finished my beer, Padre Thomas finished his and took our empties into the bar.

"Mick, you saved lives," Richard said without Thomas around. "We know it, you know it, even if the kids don't. You did good."

"Yeah," I mumbled unhappily. "Wish I could see those files, compare them with Tracy's notes."

"Coast Guard is leading the investigation, right now," he said. "Fitton and Pearlman, you need to talk to them. They'll want to talk to you soon enough to find out more about the shooting. Clear you."

He gave me his coffee cup, slapped me on the shoulder, and walked away.

Padre Thomas handed me a cold beer. He looked

concerned and I had thought he'd be glad this was over.

"Why so glum, Padre?" The cold beer tasted too good for the hour. I dragged on the cigar.

"The devil said he'd see you soon," he answered me. "That scares me."

"I killed him, he won't be seeing anyone this side of hell."

"You can't kill the devil, Mick," he said with a sour look. "He should just move on, be annoyed at you, and become someone else's problem, but he said he'd see you soon."

"And you believe him?" I took another drag on the cigar, rolled the cold beer bottle in my hand, and didn't want him to answer.

2
THE MYSTERY OF MARINA MERRICK

Heather Graham

My name is Brent Yearwood and I'm a Key West cop with the criminal division. I've recently been praised and lauded, commended and promoted. There wasn't any kind of a big shoot-out in which I gunned down drug runners or the like.

What happened was . . . .

Weird.

Then again, as people say, we live in Key West.

And weird things happen in Key West.

I was at a bar when it all began. I was off work – I never drink while I'm on duty. In truth, I'm not much of a drinker – never liked that feeling of losing control – but the Wednesday Night Cigar Smokers Club met Wednesday night at the *Oslo Bar and Grill* off Duval just a block or two south from Front Street and so I was there, nursing a local beer.

I don't smoke cigars, either, but a lot of my friends do, and having a cigar smoker's club is really just an excuse for a social hour among "saltwater Conchs, freshwater Conchs, and new fishes," the old Conchs being those few of us who are actually Key West native, freshwater Conchs being those down in Key West for seven years or more, and new fishes being Matt Garson's name for people who had just moved down.

Because of a blockade in the 1970s, Key West was momentarily a sovereign state – the Conch Republic. Matt himself is a "freshwater conch" who wishes he was a "saltwater conch." Guess we all want to be something we're not. And I think I'm trying to explain why what happened here was possible – it's just a different kind of a place.

Beyond a doubt, as the "Conch Republic" or a city in the Great State of Florida of the good old USA, Key West is a unique city. Frat parties, bachelor parties, spring break and more all occur here; when all might be quiet, we have festivals – songwriting, writing-writing, Hemingway Days, and Fantasy Fest, just to name a few. Things are crazy here, but usually laid-back crazy, and now and then bar fight crazy. But Key West is not known for its violence, but rather its history of pirates and diversity, treasure ships and sponge divers – and, of course, craziness. Hell, back in the thirties, a guy – Carl Tanzler, who called himself Count Von Cosel – managed to fall in love with a dying woman named Elena de Hoyos, convince the young beauty he could cure her of TB – didn't of course – and then stole her corpse and slept with it for seven years. Crazy – yes? Crazier – the corpse was rescued and he was brought in by the police – and then deemed *sane*. Odd, yes, but the necrophiliac hadn't killed her – he'd been in love with her and married her in death. And for seven years, somehow no one had noticed this guy buying wire and mortician's wax and perfume and other items needed to preserve – and live with – a corpse.

We have a live and let-live attitude down here, though, hey, even in Key West, the poor girl would have been sent back to her eternal rest sooner if anyone had actually known.

So, here I was off duty, just shooting the breeze with

the guys, when I went to the side bar to order another beer for Scotty Dawson when this woman walks up to me. She placed her hand on my arm and I turned and I probably froze for a good ten minutes.

You see a lot of pretty people in Key West. Tons of them. Everyone comes to Key West – but that includes a large percentage of the young and striking, male and female. I've seen gorgeous woman in nothing but body paint, blonds, brunettes, bodies in every shade known to man.

But I'd never seen anyone like her before.

She was absolutely vivid, like the burst of color that comes with fireworks, like the first sight of a full rainbow, like – the aurora borealis. Her hair was black satin streaming down around her shoulders and her eyes were the color of the royal blue paint. She was in a casual, flowing white dress that seemed to move on its own. And her face . . . sheer perfection.

I don't even think that I managed to smile. That I said a single word.

"You have to help," she said.

There was urgency in her tone. Those incredibly blue eyes of hers were filled with pleading and desperation.

I looked around; I assumed at first that a drunk was being obnoxious and trying to pick her up.

There was nothing going on at the bar. The Wednesday-night cigar smokers were involved in some kind of heavy conversation – probably solving the world hunger situation or managing the presidency – and a few couples were scattered around the wooden tables.

I found a voice at last.

"What is it miss?"

"You're a cop, right?"

"Yes – I'm off duty right now, but, of course, I'm more than happy to help you," I said, and I hoped I didn't sound like an awkward schoolboy – I felt like one.

"He's here; here in Key West."

"Who's here?" I asked. I hadn't seen a "he" in particular who might have been bothering her in any way.

Despite her beauty, I had to wonder if she'd been indulging in a few too many Key West cocktails herself.

She shook her head, that elegant mass of raven's wings hair shifting around her shoulders, shimmering almost blue-black against the soft white fabric of her dress. "Not here, not right here – but he is in Key West. And you have to stop him. Please."

"Okay, okay – who is here, and what is he going to do?"

"The Dead Time Lover is here – in Key West. And, he's going to kill again."

I again wondered if she'd had a few too many libations – Blue Moon Splendor was the signature cocktail here.

I knew about the killer they were calling the Dead Time Killer – "they" as in the media. The police, of course, were – to the best of my knowledge – protesting the giving of a moniker to the killer that could only please him. He was becoming infamous – taking his place among the annals of serial killers.

Thing is, he'd been killing nowhere near Florida, much less Key West. He'd taken victims in New England and New York City.

A creeping sensation suddenly seemed to encompass me like an unseen fog. It was strange – damned strange that she was bringing him up here – in Key West.

The Dead Time Lover seemed to be taking a page from that story I mentioned earlier – except that so far, he had been New England and New York crazy.

Not quite the same. The Dead Time Lover picked up his victims in bars. He lured them out somewhere, strangled them – and then kept the bodies for days. He'd sent a number of letters to the police and media – telling him that he loved his girls and he knew that they loved him, but there had been only so long that love seemed to last.

There were five victims so far – each had eventually been found in a dark alley, days after their deaths – laid out with their hair combed and their arms crossed over their chests – and flowers placed by them. Tracing clues in his four-month killing spree had been problematic; each victim had been abducted in a different suburb or neighborhood and left in a totally different location, involving police forces from different cities and states and the FBI as well.

It was summer, so the victims were being found pretty quickly – even in New England.

Apparently, the Dead Time Lover didn't have Carl Tanzler's ability to preserve a corpse.

Naturally, the case had national attention, but it wasn't a local case in any way and while I'm sure there were details the police involved with each death knew, I wasn't in on the particulars.

But this woman before me – this beautiful young woman – seemed to be convinced that she knew something – and had seen the killer.

"Were you approached; do you know who this man is?" I asked her, trying to spring back into cop mode. I admit, I was a little off. The evening had been about beer and cigars and discussions on the best dive boat, Grady Miller's penchant for chocolate, and the state of the world at large – and this startling beauty, touching me, coming to me.

"What makes you think that the Dead Time Lover has come here?" I asked her.

"I've seen him. I'm certain that it is him. You have to stop him," she said. "He's here – down at the south end of

Duval. I saw him. He's trolling – he'll be at a bar at the end of Duval. He's trying to seduce a woman. You can save her; you have a chance. You can save her."

She seemed to be sincere – passionately sincere.

"Miss, please, I'm going to need a little more. First, who are you?" I asked. "How do you know who he is? Can you come with me to the station? You can tell us everything you know; the Dead Time Lover has been in the far northeast and this is – "

She turned away from me. I caught her arm to stop her. She was really scared; she felt just as cold as ice and those eyes of hers . . . .

"I was afraid you wouldn't listen," she said softly.

"I'm listening, Miss – Miss – "

"Marina," she told me, and smiled. "My name is Marina." She looked at me with those huge blue eyes. "Trust me; I'm begging you to trust me."

"Forgive me. I've just met you. At a bar," I pointed out. "I need more information."

"You don't need information. I can't go with you to the station. There's no time. Just come with me. I can find him for you. We can save her. Please."

I glanced at the table and saw that the guys were all watching me.

I figured it was with envy. This girl was beyond beautiful. And they were thinking that I was a lucky dog. I'm the youngest of this crew at twenty-six, and I cut a fair figure being a good six-three and pretty fit. As to my face – it seems to be arranged okay.

But, I was a still a little humbled by this beauty.

"Hey, you coming back here, or what, Yearwood?" Crusty old Sam Normandy called out to me.

I looked back at Marina Merrick and those pleading eyes.

Yeah, it was a cop matter, and I was off duty, but if

those guys thought I'd go back to them with a woman like this looking at me, asking for my help . . . .

"May or may not be back!" I called to Sam, and to Marina, I said, "Let's go." I remembered what I'd been doing at the bar. "Send Scotty another beer; put it on my tab," I said, raising my voice so that Ted Neil, owner and operator of the fine rustic establishment, would get Scotty his drink.

With Marina clinging to my arm, we headed out to Duval. It was a Wednesday night, not a weekend, and there was no festival going on, so the street was only at a medium roar. Music – good music! – streamed from the Irish bar. It was summer and hot – but a great breeze was coming off the water, as it often was.

"Great place, if you haven't been there," I told Marina, inclining my head toward the Irish bar.

"I was there – just once," she told me. "A few years ago. And I did enjoy it."

"So, where are you from?" I asked her. *New England? Was that why she was certain she was watching some guy who might be the Dead Time Lover? New York City?*

To the best of my knowledge, there hadn't even been any sketches of the fellow out there – forensic specialists were busy trying to determine if the letters that had come in to the police and the media were real – or from some crazy wanna-be. You'd think, with five victims, in today's day and age, he would have messed up somewhere by now. Left a fingerprint, a skin cell, something.

But they were working blindly, tracing down the victims. Plying friends for information.

They had nothing.

"Atlanta – Georgia," she told me. She had been so tense – almost driven. But she looked at me then, and actually smiled. "You dive right?"

"Sure. I grew up here."

"Well, I'm new, but I love to dive. I came down to Miami for a bachelorette party, but I was so excited for the opportunity to dive. Just wasn't as into the partying as I should have been, I guess. You know, my friends wanted to stay out – I wanted to be sober and clear-headed for diving. Anyway . . . thank you. Thank you for coming with me now."

"Of course," I murmured.

I couldn't help but wonder if this wasn't some bachelorette party game. *Everyone has to find a cop and trick him into doing something. Seduce him – into being a fool.*

"Miami, huh?" I said.

"Gateway to the Keys!" she told me.

We were walking quickly. Some drunk jerk almost plowed right into her as we passed St. Paul's Church. I pulled her close to me.

It was okay if a game was being played on me. It had been a few months since Jill and I had broken up and she'd left Key West for the cowboys of Montana. It felt good to hold her, to pull her close and protect her.

"There's a few in every crowd," she murmured.

Kiosks with vendors were still out on the sidewalks and late night diners were busy enjoying restaurants.

"Have you been to the *Hardrock* here?" I asked her. "It's haunted, of course," I added with a smile. "Rich dude hanged himself there," I told her, nodding with my inside knowledge.

Why the hell was I giving a travel monologue? I was a good cop. She seemed to be convinced someone was going to be killed. I was going to stop it . . . .

Or be the brunt of a terrific joke.

"Marina," I said – since my arm was protectively around her now, it seemed okay to use her given name, "You have to help me out here now. What makes you think this is the guy? The Dead Time Lover?"

"I believe I've seen him in action," she murmured.

"In Boston? In New York?" I asked.

She looked at me with grave eyes. "A member of our bachelorette party disappeared in Miami; she's still just listed as a missing person. The cops were good; they tried to help. But she just disappeared – right off of South Beach."

My heart skipped a beat.

Then logic settled in. Missing person cases were never taken lightly – but there were often other answers than the assumption of foul play. Adults sometimes wanted to disappear. Young women sometimes disappeared with young men for days – only to reappear astounded that people were worried about them.

"Marina," I reminded her, "even Miami is far, far from New England and New York. Are you sure that your friend didn't just – make a new friend and go off?"

"I'm certain," she said.

Okay, so I knew what I was dealing with. Marina was positive that her friend would have called her – or someone – if she had gone off. Bad things happened the world over – the Dead Time Lover didn't have to be involved. If I remember some of my seminars correctly, behavior analysts believe that there are at least twenty and possibly several hundred serial killers at work in just the United States alone at any given time.

Survivor's guilt.

She'd seen someone who looked like someone who had been at a South Beach bar when she'd last seen her friend.

And that was okay.

I was off duty. I could go with her – and ease her mind.

And maybe after . . . .

We'd at least have a drink. And maybe . . . well, it was Key West, who knew?

Except, of course, that she was the kind of woman who would stay with you forever, haunt you memory and your dreams and . . . .

Hey, she was a diver. Maybe she could be convinced to move to my island paradise.

How ridiculous and sad were my fantasies? I'd just met her . . . and I wasn't sure if she was sane, or if she was stringing me along on a challenge or a prank.

"There – there's where I saw him last," she said.

She pointed across the street. We were near the Butterfly Conservatory and the "Southernmost Hotel," though with property changes and even land mass changes, I'm not so sure it's still technically southernmost.

There was a new place on the corner. *Josie's*. Strange what businesses do and don't make it in Key West. Some bars have been around forever. Take *Captain Tony's* or *Sloppy Joe's*. Others, they seem to change on a daily basis.

Josie's had been there for a couple of months and seemed to be going strong. They had a big old structure that had been used once in the sponging business and was now just – big. The owners had set it up with a good stage and an amazing sound system. They brought in local bands that were right on the verge of making it big. They kept their kitchen open until two in the morning while offering different drink specials on the hour. Each book of server tabs came with one sheet that was starred – and the lucky person or group had their entire tab picked up.

Josie's just might make it – if they kept up the marketing.

"In there," I murmured, eyeing the place.

Two bouncers were at the open front doors. They'd been decked out to fit the Keys with dual palm trees in big pots alongside the bouncers. Palm fronds decorated the opening and the windows.

From where we were, I could hear the band – seemed like a decent group tonight doing a bang-up job with a cover of a Bon Jovi tune.

And it was busy. Wednesday night, yes. But this place seemed to be swelling with whatever tourist population had fled mid-week to the Keys.

"I saw him," she said. "Please. At the least . . . watch him, let me show you . . . I know I saw him in Miami."

"At a distance, from across the room – "

"Up close and personal," she said. "Please. He was there – right before the disappearance."

We went in. I knew Joey Giralda, the bouncer on the left. He nodded at me. "Hey, the cigar club thing losing its lure?" he teased.

Joey was a good guy. We'd gone to school together. We were both still in Key West.

I inclined my head to Marina with a shrug.

Joey arched a brow. I was sure he was wondering how I had managed to snare such a beauty.

"Thought I'd see how this place was doing," I told him.

"Going strong!" Joey said.

Marina tugged my arm. We walked on in. I looked down again into those endless blue eyes.

Prank or not, I was in.

Much of the large area was dance floor or standing around room. The band was on a stage to the left; drummer, rhythm guitar, lead guitar, bass, keyboard player, and a saxophonist. Nice. I found that I paused a minute to watch them.

Marina tugged at my arm again. "We have to start looking," she said. "It's getting late!"

It was growing late, I realized. A little past midnight, at any rate. Not *really* late – not by Key standards. But, hey, when she looked at me . . . .

I moved on with her. Couples were dancing; groups were just hanging out together, laughing, talking. Most were tourists; I didn't see any more friends.

Around the walls, tables were set up – rustic wood tables, perfect for the keys. The bar – extending along most of the western edge of the building – was made of old ship's planking. Nautical pictures graced the walls. Sharks, tropical scenes, boats . . . a few silhouettes of couples romantically wandering down the beach at sunset.

"Anything?" I asked her. I looked around, trying to see if there was a group of young women somewhere near, giggling, ready to see the cop that Marina had snared.

I didn't see such a group.

"He was at the bar earlier," she said a little desperately.

"Then I'll get us some drinks," I told her.

"I'll nab that little high top table there," she said. "We can see the dance floor and the bar from there."

"Perfect. What would like?"

She smiled. "Water," she told me.

She gave me something almost like a pained smile and pointed to one of the high top tables near the bar. They had cool, tree like stands and the seats were made of the same wood. Nice.

At the bar I figured I'd get another beer to sip at – bartenders weren't all that fond of you when you ordered two waters. I didn't know the fellow who served me – he had an Eastern European accent.

"Romanian?" I asked him, trying to be friendly.

"Albanian," he told me

"Welcome to Key West," I said. He nodded, happy with the tip I left.

I started to make my way through the crowd nudging its way to the bar but then stopped – I'll never know why I stopped, but I did, my attention drawn to a couple who had snared a few of the bar stools.

She was pretty; a blond with big brown eyes. He was a good-looking man – rather thin but aesthetic face, sandy hair, and a beach-boy smile. They were laughing and chatting – and drinking the bar special – "Key Coconuts!" – made from coconut and pineapple and a shot of every bar liquor and served in a coconut shell.

Potent drinks, I thought. And, being a Key West cop, my first thought was, *I hope to hell that neither of them is driving anywhere!*

Then, of course, since I had paused, I looked down the length of the bar.

Three middle-aged men at the end of the bar, eyeing one of the dancers out on the floor, a lovely young inebriated thing in short-shorts and endowed with massive breast that gyrated with each of her twisted movements. Next to them, a duo of young women, unaware of anything else but their own conversation. Next, a couple who appeared to be in their late thirties – maybe a married couple on a bit of an escape. The kids would be home in a hotel room, the oldest sibling in charge or perhaps with a babysitter – available through most major hotels and other venues.

Next to them . . . .

A twenty-something brunette next to a drop-dead GQ stud. He was earnestly trying to convince her of something.

She pointed to the two girls down the bar. I couldn't hear their conversation clearly, but she had raised her voice to be above the music and the din in the bar.

"I'm here with my friends!" I heard.

Something seemed to crawl along my flesh. The guy didn't look like a serial killer who liked to sleep with corpses – but then, to the best of my knowledge, no one had ever clearly described such an individual.

I edged closer to them, listening.

"Of course," GQ stud said. "Look, I'll talk to Mary tomorrow. The shoot is just the two of us, but Marty might be able to do a beach scene. It's for the new Elizabeth Oliver line of clothing. Marty is the executive in charge. If he says we can get them in, we can get them in."

He indicated the men at the end of the bar – the older men who were googling the short-shorts girl with the Oscar-worthy dancing breasts.

"Marty!" the man called out.

The old guy looked at him. "Can we do a group shot – use a few hot extras tomorrow?"

Marty wasn't to be distracted. He didn't even look over at GQ stud.

"Whatever!" he called back.

I realized I was standing there like a voyeur; the whole thing looked legitimate enough. GQ stud did seem to be the kind of a guy you'd choose for a modeling shoot. And no one was trying to get anyone to go anywhere.

I made my way to the high top table where Marina, beyond beautiful, awaited me.

She didn't look at me as I set her water and my beer down on the table.

"You saw him!" she said.

"That's not him, Marina," I told her. "That guy is with the older men at the end of the table. The woman he's talking to must be a model, too. And she's here with the two girls there. And none of them appears to be leaving."

She looked at me then, amazed that I could be so blind. Then she shook her head.

"No, no, not that guy – the other one!"

She pointed to the man who was part of the first duo I had noticed. The fellow with the beach boy look and aesthetic face – the one sitting with the pretty blond as they both enjoyed their coconut drinks.

Even as I looked, they both rose.

"She's going with him; he'll kill her," she told me.

"Marina – "

"Please! I'll stay here – you're a cop. Just follow them. Follow them at a distance. Watch where they go; he'll take her somewhere dark. And he'll have a van parked somewhere near. Please, I'm begging you – go!"

I figured I'd humor her. Maybe, when I followed them, someone would jump out of the bushes and laugh and tell me I'd been "punked."

But . . . .

I was in lust. No, lust was wrong. I was totally enchanted. Not that I wasn't in lust . . . but, it was those eyes of hers that seduced me, the sound of her voice, and the brush of her fingers.

"Please!" she begged me. "Hurry!"

"Okay, but there are laws, you know. And I am a cop – more subject to the law than your average guy because I'm supposed to know it. If they just pull out a key and enter a hotel room . . . ."

"Go!"

And so I did.

I know how to shadow people. I'm good at it. Last year, I was the cop who nailed the guy who had been heisting purses and bags – a truly gifted thief. I thread through the crowd and caught the bastard red-handed. I followed the couple who had been doing a bang up job of ripping off rental properties along Roosevelt and caught them trying to sell the stolen goods. I know the island like the back of my hand – every nook and cranny. I looked like a guy on a bachelor-party mission and it seems that pickpockets and con artists don't realize I'm a threat – until the cuffs are out.

Thing is, it was late. I had to be ultra-careful. While *Josie's* was still doing a fair amount of business, the area –

almost a mile from Front Street and the hub of late-night establishments in that area – was growing quiet. There was no crowd on the sidewalks in which to hide in plain sight.

I had to keep my distance from them. It seemed, however, that they were heading back to the more populated area. That was good.

I let them get a good block ahead of me. Of course, I was wary – waiting for that moment when someone stepped out of a doorway or from around the corner to tell me I was great chump.

But no one did.

I glanced at my watch beneath a streetlight; nearly 1:00 A.M.

The ghost tours had finished for the night; those hearty souls still up and about wouldn't be on the side streets of the city.

But my quarry was still headed toward Front Street. His arm was around her; she was leaning against him. He seemed to be moving her along easily enough.

Straight, straight, straight. I could even hear the music now, coming the Irish bar or maybe Sloppy Joe's.

Then suddenly, they turned off at Eaton Street, right by the church.

I was a block behind; I quickened my pace.

When I turned the corner, there was no one to be seen. A few hours earlier, and I might have encountered a ghost tour. The graveyard here is supposed to be the final resting place for an old sea captain and a group of children killed in a terrible fire in an old theater across the street. It's dark and there's a parking lot and lots of quiet areas where . . . .

A woman's scream would be heard! I told myself.

True.

Maybe.

If that woman were able to scream!

46

I walked as quietly as I could myself, turning the corner, hurrying by the church, reaching the fenced in section of the graveyard. I saw no one; I could have kept on going straight but I thought about that parking lot, surrounded by trees and brush and foliage.

I hurried along the side of the side of the graveyard and that's when I heard her.

She wasn't screaming.

She was gasping and choking and . . . .

I ran. I ran into that parking area and discovered that he had her backed up to the graveyard fence – close to that monument to the long dead seafarer – and he was choking the life out of her.

I didn't stop to think then to be amazed.

Or even to note the off-white van legally parked so close to the lot.

I simply reacted. I went into cop mode and came at him straight from the back, using a high-school wrestling move to drag him off her and down to the ground.

He was a lean fellow – with an aesthetic face.

And a beach boy smile, of course.

Not much of a fighter, not when met with a stronger force.

"Hey!" he protested in a howl, as I rolled him on the parking lot pavement to get plastic cuffs on him. "Hey, we were just getting a little kinky. Didn't you see *Fifty Shades*, my friend?"

"*Fifty Shades*!" the young blond gasped. "He was killing me!"

She had fallen to the ground by the fence. Her hand was at her throat. Tears were spilling from her eyes.

I began my cop-legal-litany to the man on the ground, breaking off to assure the blond that help was on its way. And it was – quickly. I can speed-dial the department before you can blink.

Like I said, I'm a good cop.

Within minutes, sirens were blazing. An ambulance came for the girl who was, yes, definitely going to press charges.

But was this guy really the Dead Time Lover? Could he be?

I began to worry about Marina. By the time all the brass and EMTs were involved, it was closer to morning than it was the-night-before.

I had to go to the station; I had made the collar. I had paper work. I managed, however, to excuse myself long enough to call *Josie's* and ask a bartender to find Marina and just tell her that I'd be there as soon as possible; the bartender told me he'd try and hung up.

By the time it was all done, I knew that even *Josie's* had closed.

I figured that she'd find me the next day – after all, she had found me the first time.

It had all happened in such a bizarre – and paperwork filled – manner that it wasn't until the sun was near to coming up that I got a chance to explain to my lieutenant that it hadn't been happenstance that I'd been there, and that I'd been tipped off by a young woman. And I remembered then about the van and told him that I'd forgotten to check out in the midst of the arrest and the EMTs helping the victim – turned out that the young woman nearly had been strangled; she'd bear bruises around her neck along with her sunburn for the next week, at the least.

The guy I arrested was John Martin. Nothing seemed remarkable about him – or his name. He kept claiming that he was just after a little asphyxiation, a little kinky sex.

I didn't check out the van; the lieutenant sent other cops to do that. I went home and went to bed.

My place is on Whitehead, an old house my family had bought in the 1930s. My parents had retired – to Arizona. Go figure.

I live alone. It's a little shotgun house.

I'm close friends with my partner, Beth. There's nothing romantic between us – Beth is married to a great girl. I love them both. They assure me all the time that if they were ever to find anything attractive about a man, it would be me. I know it's never happening.

But Beth is accustomed to banging on my door whenever she feels like it.

And she felt like it at 8:30 A.M.

I groaned, protesting as I heard her voice. I walked to the door and opened it in my skivvies – I knew they did nothing for Beth, but hey, she'd woken me up.

She didn't notice what I was wearing.

"Beth, hell, I'm supposed to get a day today because – "

"Because last night you caught the Dead Time Lover!" she exclaimed.

I was glad that she rushed me with a huge hug – I do mean huge. Beth is about five-ten inches of lean, wiry strength.

I pulled back from her, frowning. "It really was the Dead Time Lover? How do they know? I mean, for sure. And you mean . . . you mean that it really was him? But they didn't know his name, or what he looked like. And he'd been killing women far from here and – "

"Oh, man, are you kidding me?" Beth demanded. "The FBI agents here were in the station and stuff was shooting back and forth with their offices in New York and the northeast since you left. They found all kinds of stuff in the bastard's van – things that belonged to the other victims! Purses – shoes! He's being shipped off with the Feds as we speak. My man, my partner! You caught the Dead Time

Lover. And you're mine – all mine! Love my partner!"

And she hugged me and kissed me on the cheek again.

"I got to get in there; I'm not sure I believe this myself," I told her.

She talked the whole time I dressed; I could hear her going on and on as I got ready. The cops would be able to verify it; law enforcement did have DNA – saliva left on the breast of one of his victims. They were pretty sure that by evening, they'd have proof beyond a doubt that the man they held was the killer. He'd left the fertile killing ground of the northeast section of the country to come south.

And he could do so easily – take a nice slow ride south in the summer – because he was a teacher!

It was all true. When I reached the station, everyone looked at me with amazement. Everyone congratulated me. I was going to be commended, I'd be up for a promotion.

I was the man.

I tried to explain to them all what had happened. I told them that a young woman had tipped me off. A beautiful dark-haired woman named Marina.

I was the object of a press conference. I told everyone that I'd had a tip-off from a young woman named Marina; if they saw her, they should please tell her I said thank you and that I was looking forward to seeing her again.

The press conference was solemn. The Dead Time Lover had killed five women. There were still some smiles when I said I'd like to see the young woman again and one of the reporters told me that she was sure a number of young women would like to see me.

I was riding high.

And aching for Marina. I thought she might show up at the station. It would be easy for her to find me – I was the man of the hour.

I realized I'd never even pressed for her last name.

That night, I went back to the *Oslo Bar and Grill*, hoping against hope that Marina would be there or that she had been there and maybe left me a note.

Matt, Scotty, and Sam were there, at their usual table.

I joined them. The three rose and lifted their beer bottles to me and did an embarrassing bowing thing.

"Quit, quit!" I begged them. "He was a scrawny thing – man, I didn't even get a bruise from it. And I wouldn't have gotten him if it hadn't been for Marina. I'm trying to find her. Have you seen her?"

"Her?" Sam said, furrowing white brows as thick as a bird's wings.

"Marina?" Matt asked.

"The girl I left with – the girl I met at the bar," I said, aggravated. How the hell had any one of them missed her?

Sandy shook his head. "Missed her – you high-tailed it out of here like a kite."

Aggravated, I went to the bar. The bartender didn't remember her either.

I think I left Sam, Sandy, and Matt in a huff, but I was growing a little desperate. I headed down to *Josie's*. My friend Joey was off – on vacation and wouldn't be back for two weeks.

The bartender from the night before shook his head. He didn't know who I was talking about, either. He reminded me that I'd come to the bar alone.

Of course. I'd left Marina at the high top table.

It wasn't until the next morning that Beth – partner and bosom buddy Beth – arrived at my house again, banging at the door. I was back on duty. But, I wasn't late. I was not in the best of moods. I couldn't believe that Marina had disappeared.

She burst in the door with a newspaper – a real newspaper in black and white print (with color ads, of course.)

"Brent!" she said.

"What?"

"This girl – this Marina who gave you the tip – what did you say she looked like?"

"Like Snow White," I said. "The fairest of the fair! Blue eyes, black hair, luscious skin."

"Like this?" Beth asked softly.

She handed me the paper. And there, on the front page, was Marina's picture. It was a beautiful picture – of a beautiful woman. She was laughing; her head was cast back. All that was gorgeous and glorious about her seemed to shine through on the page.

Merrick. Her name had been Merrick. Marina Merrick.

I read the headline.

"Last of the Dead Time Lover's victims discovered in Miami alley."

"No!" I said. "No!" I thrust the paper from me as if the paper itself were evil – as if the headline lied.

"Brent, I love you like my brother; you're the best partner ever. But you gotta stop telling people that this girl was with you, and that she sent you after the killer. Brent! They just found her – she'd been dead *over a week* when you claimed that she was with you!"

I'm not a pansy – honest to God, I'm not.

Hell, I'm a Southern boy.

I dropped into a dead faint.

Thank God, Beth was the only one to see me as I fell.

(And strong enough to catch me before I bashed my head in.)

So, I quit talking about it.

The pretty blond girl I'd saved came to see me when she was out of the hospital. She was Deanna Bolton, down from Jacksonville, and she was going to take a job with a marine research facility in Key West. She'd almost headed back to Jacksonville – but with cops like me in Key West, she decided to stay.

I told her I was glad. We were a little awkward. She was very attractive and sweet – and shell-shocked and punch drunk.

I was still in love.

Maybe, in time, we'll start seeing one another.

Actually, I think we will.

For now, I'm back to the Wednesday Night Cigar Smoker's Club.

I was sitting there, still just thinking about Marina, when old Sam tapped me on the hand.

Old Sam is a true conch. His father was born in Key West; his father's father was born in Key West.

"You okay, son?" he asked me.

"Doing fine, Sam, doing fine," I told him.

He nodded, and then said, "You'll be all right. You'll be all right. Give it a little time. But, you'll be all right. Because you know."

"Okay, thanks," I said. "Sam, what is it that I know."

He nodded sagely at me. "It's Key West, son," he told me.

"Yeah?"

Old Sam shrugged.

"Weird things happen here, so. It's Key West – and weird things happen here."

He lifted his beer bottle to me.

I returned the gesture.

Because, of course, he was right.

3.
LAST CHANCE

Bill Craig

Lew Carroll looked at the cards in his hands and folded. His streak of bad luck continued. "I'm out," he said. Grabbing the nearly empty glass of whiskey he pushed away from the table and headed for the bar. Lew Carroll was on a downhill slide. He still had his looks, thick brown hair streaked with blond from the tropical sun, blue eyes and his West Texas twang. Except tonight, his blue eyes were bloodshot and red-rimmed from exhaustion. His light gray linen blazer hung limply over his pale blue dress shirt that was starting to fray around the collar. He dug into his pocket and pulled out a pack of Camel cigarettes.

Carroll slipped onto a seat at the bar and sat down his glass, shaking out a cigarette, he stuck it in the corner of his mouth and pulled out a battered silver Zippo lighter and flipped it open and dragged his thumb across the striker wheel igniting a pale yellow and blue flame. He touched the end of the Camel to the flame, drawing the fire up into the tobacco, feeling the burn as he pulled the hot smoke into his throat and lungs. Carroll snapped the lighter closed and dropped it back in his pants' pocket. He picked up his glass after exhaling and drained it, then held it up so that the pretty bartender could bring him another.

His run of bad luck had started in Memphis. A big loss and then the raid by the cops. Lew was pretty sure that

Garner had set the whole thing up, but as he had been told to get out of town, things didn't get any better. Even in small pick-up games in small bars heading south, his luck refused to turn. Most days he barely broke even. He was beginning to think that his life as a professional gambler was drawing to a close. If he couldn't get his luck to turn, he'd have to give it up. Then he heard about the big Key West poker tournament. A high stakes game, winner take all.

Maybe his last chance. And where better for it to be than the place known as the end of the road.

The bartender brought him a fresh drink and sat it on the polished wood in front of him. He thanked her and took a sip, enjoying the burn. Lew smiled to himself. He sipped his whiskey to keep control, both of his drinking and so that others would think he had imbibed more than he had. It kept him sharper. He looked around the bar. It was getting late and the place had thinned out. The bartender moved down to the other end of the bar. Lew Carroll surveyed the room.

That's when he saw her. Sitting alone in a quiet corner, her red hair gleaming beneath the neon glare of a window sign. She was wearing a well-made black dress and heels, a small black bag on the table beside her. A nearly empty martini sat on the table in front of her. Lew got the bartender's attention and sent a martini over to the table. He stubbed out his cigarette in a handy ashtray. He took another sip of his own drink before he became aware of a presence at his elbow. Carroll half turned in his seat. It was the redhead.

"I wanted to say thank you," she told him in a sultry voice that was sweeter than a marshmallow soaked in honey. There was a trace of the Deep South in her voice. South Carolina or maybe Georgia, he thought. She was older than he had originally thought, perhaps late thirties instead of early thirties. There were a few laugh lines starting to show around her eyes and smile lines at the corners of luscious red lips. A single strand of white pearls adorned her neck. God had blessed her with s sprinkling of freckles across a slightly up-turned nose. Her eyes were blue and intelligent.

"You're welcome," Lew said, finally finding his voice. "You looked lonely sitting there."

"Really? My date never showed up," she said.

"He was very foolish then," Lew told her.

"I really hate drinking alone," she said. Lew nodded and grabbed his glass, following her back to her table. He appreciated the gentle sway of her heart-shaped ass as she seemed to almost float across the floor. He put his drink on the table and helped her with her chair, a sudden flash of chivalry that he had long thought forgotten, then he took the seat across from her.

"I know this sounds like a bad movie line, but what's a nice girl like you doing in a place like this?" Lew asked. He had already examined her left hand. No wedding band there. Nor a white line showing where one had been removed. She rewarded him with a wan smile.

"It does sound like a bad movie line, but the question is a good one nonetheless," the young woman replied. "I came down from Miami on a job. I was supposed to have a date tonight, but he never showed," she shrugged.

"Do you have a name?" Lew asked, intensely curious about the quiet, yet vivacious young woman sitting across from him.

"Sarah. Sarah Clark," she replied. "I'm sorry, I should have introduced myself, Mr. ...?" she let the unfinished sentence hang there.

"Carroll, Lew Carroll. I forgot my own manners, Sarah," Lew replied.

"Why did you buy me the drink, Lew?" Sarah asked,

genuine curiosity in her voice.

"You looked lonely, sitting here by yourself. It was, I don't know, a gesture I guess. Something to let you know you weren't alone after all," he shrugged.

"And now I'm not," Sarah smiled. This time it wasn't wan, this time it was a full-blown smile that seemed to light up her whole face.

"No, now you're not," he smiled at her.

"So why did you stay here alone after it became obvious your date wasn't coming?" Lew asked. He took another sip of his drink. He dug out his cigarettes and offered her one. Sarah reached over and took it, her eyes never leaving his as he dragged out his lighter and lit it for her. Then he lit his own. The cigarette seemed to relax the girl and he was glad of it. She leaned back in her chair.

"Because I was lonely. This job, well let's just say it wasn't what I thought it was going to be," Sarah shrugged. She took a sip of her drink.

"They were fools then," Lew said, meaning it.

"Life is a crapshoot much of the time," Sarah shook her head.

"It is," he agreed.

"Do you always go around helping damsels in distress?"

"Rarely," he told her.

"What do you do, Lew?"

"Usually I gamble. Professional poker player," Lew shrugged.

"Can I trust you?" Sarah looked into his eyes.

"As much as anybody, I guess," Lew shrugged.

"Will you do me a favor?"

"Sure, in for a penny in for a pound," he shrugged.

"My Dad used to say that," Sarah grinned.

"Ouch," Lew winced. Sarah reached into her bag and took out a small package wrapped in plain brown paper and tied with string. She slid it across the table to him. There was an address written on it in slanting cursive strokes.

"Hold this for a couple of days for me. Then drop it in the mail. Will you do that?" Sarah asked.

"What's this about? He asked.

"Remember that job I told you about?"

"Sure," Lew nodded. Picking up the small package, he slipped it into his jacket pocket. Sarah stubbed out her cigarette and finished her drink. She stood and leaned over and kissed his cheek.

"Thank you, Lew," she said, turning and walking out. Lew sat there a second then tossed back what was left of his whiskey and staggered after her.

Outside the night air was warm and humid, slapping him across the face like a wet blanket. Lew looked around but the girl was gone. The crowd was thinning out as the night wound down. But of the girl, there was no sign. She had vanished like a ghost, a spectral being that was there for a heartbeat and gone the next. Shaking his head, he started walking to his hotel.

Bright sunlight streaming in through his window awakened him. Lew Carroll rolled to a sitting position on the edge of the bed. What a night. It still seemed so surreal that he wasn't sure that it had actually happened. He headed for the shower.

Half an hour later he was seated at Harpoon Harry's eating breakfast and perusing the latest edition of the Key West Citizen. The more he read the more he decided that the island suffered from a special breed of insanity. Ron, the manager had greeted him when he entered and flitted around from table to table, checking on the guests in his establishment.

Then a small item inside caught his eye. A young

woman had been run down the night before not far from the bar where he had been playing cards. The police were calling it a deliberate hit and run. Her identity was being withheld pending notification of family.

Suddenly Lew was no longer hungry. He thought about the encounter the night before. It was then he had remembered the small package she had given him. It was still in his coat pocket, back in his room. He wondered if it had anything to do with her being run down. If it had been her.

Lew shook his head, digging his crumpled pack of Camels from the brightly colored Hawaiian Aloha shirt he was wearing. His hands were trembling as he shook one free and stuck it in the corner of his mouth. He got the pack back in his pocket and dug out his lighter and fired the smoke up. He had already paid for his meal and left it sitting as he walked out into the bright sunshine. A cool breeze was blowing in off the Gulf, pushing the humidity back, but doing little against the oppressive heat. Lew slipped on a pair of dark-lensed sunglasses as he tried to decide where he wanted to go.

He had to find out more about the girl, had to know if it had been Sarah who had been run down like a dog on the street. He had liked her. She had touched something deep inside him, something that he had thought long dead. His heart.

Lew walked down to the police station on Roosevelt Blvd. He hesitated on the steps. He had no proof that the dead girl was Sarah Clark. It was just a suspicion on his part. There was a good chance the cops wouldn't believe him. Lew sighed. He had to try. He pushed the glass door open and stepped inside.

White tiles and white walls greeted him, stretching off in both directions. A brown door with the words information stenciled on it stood a few steps away. Carroll shrugged and walked over to it, his hand grabbing the gold knob and turning it. He pushed the door open and stepped inside.

A long counter bisected the room and there were three nice looking women behind it. Lew walked up to the counter, waiting on one of them to notice him. He stood there for a couple of minutes before clearing his throat loudly. Finally a Hispanic woman turned her chair to face him.

"Can I help you?" she asked, a slight accent tinting the words.

"I want to talk to somebody about the woman that was killed in the hit and run last night. I think I might know her," Lew managed to get it out without stammering.

"I think Sgt. Ortiz caught that one. Hold on a second and I'll call him and let him know you are here," she smiled at him, turning and pressing a button on her phone. She spoke quietly for a moment and then paused to listen. Finally she hung up and turned back to face him. "Sgt. Ortiz is sending down Alvarez and Jones to escort you up."

"Thanks," Lew told her. He started to dig out a cigarette before he noticed the no smoking sign. Shit. He took a seat in one of the plastic chairs and picked up the latest copy of Sports Illustrated. He was thumbing through it when the door opened and two men stepped into the room.

One was dark with Latino good looks, the other a kind of grungy looking blond with a barely there mustache. Both were wearing expensive suits. "Mr. Carroll?" the Latino asked. Lew nodded and stood extending his hand. It seemed the polite thing to do.

"I'm Detective Alvarez. My partner, Detective Jones. You say you may know our vic from the hit and run?"

"Maybe. I met a young woman named Sarah Clark in the Smoking Tuna last night. We shared a drink and she left. She was about medium height, curvaceous and had red hair. She left a few seconds before me and by the time I got outside she was gone,' Carroll told them.

"What was she wearing, this Sarah Clark?" Detective Jones asked.

"An expensive black dress and white pearls, black pumps and a handbag," Lew replied.

"She have a bag?"

"A small one. What's going on guys?" Lew asked.

"Her bag was missing. But you just described our murder victim," Alvarez said.

"I was afraid of that," Lew sighed.

"Why is that?" Jones asked him.

"There was something about her, I don't know, a sense of loneliness. Like she was alone and afraid," Lew replied. He really wished he could have a cigarette.

"Turns out she was," Jones said.

"Who did this to her?" Lew looked at them both.

"That is what we want to find out," Alvarez said. Alvarez gave him a card and Lew Carroll tucked it into his pocket. Alvarez walked him to the door.

"Thank you," Lew Carroll told him.

"No, thank you, Mr. Carroll. You have given us the best lead we have," Alvarez told him. Lew nodded and then turned and headed back along Roosevelt Blvd to where it intersected with Duval. He had a game to set up. It was a prelim to get into the big game.

Lew Carroll finally won a big hand at the Hog's Breath. It was a back room game, but the stakes were fair. Lew was glad to see it happen. Maybe his luck was finally starting to change. He raked in the chips and tossed a couple of high ones to the dealer.

By 6 p.m., Lew Carroll was up by a thousand dollars. He bowed out of the game, hoping to keep his streak alive. He cashed in his winnings and walked back to his hotel.

The sun was setting as he unlocked the door of his room. Lew Carroll closed the door behind him, hearing the lock click shut. His gray jacket was still hanging where he had left it. He walked to the closet and fished out the brown paper-wrapped package. Lew weighed it in his hand as he looked as the pre-paid postage.

Lew thought about opening it, just to see what might be inside, but decided against it. He owed her that much. Lew looked at the name on the package, the name of the person she was sending it too. Carol Doyle. Carol appeared to live in Miami. Lew wondered about that. What made this address special? He shook his head.

Was it worth a trip to Miami to find out? Or should he just do what Sarah had asked of him and hold onto it for another day before mailing it. At that moment, his phone rang. The sound was unexpected and so jarringly loud he dropped the package and nearly fell down. He moved around the bed and picked it up by the third ring.

"Hello?" he said, having no idea who would be calling him.

"You have something that belongs to me," a menacing voice told him.

"Who are you?" Lew asked, sweat suddenly beading on his forehead, despite the cold air blasting from the air-conditioner.

"Who I am doesn't matter, Mr. Carroll. What matters is the package that Sarah gave you. It belongs to me," the voice told him. It was deep and hollow sounding, reminding him of Darth Vader, a character from a movie he had watched as a kid.

"Sarah?" Lew decided to play it cagey.

"The young woman you bought a drink for last night,

and then inquired about at the police station today." Shit! The guy on the other end of the line was good.

"Oh yeah, the redhead," Lew replied, swallowing hard.

"I know you have the package because her bag was empty. I know she gave it to you," the voice said. Lew's stomach was practically rolling now.

"Bring it to me tonight, after the sunset crowd thins out from Mallory Square. Stand by the sea wall. One of my people will come to you." The line went dead. Lew put the phone down and immediately grabbed his crumpled pack of smokes. He pulled the last one out of the pack and stuck it in his mouth. He balled the empty cigarette package in his fist and threw it at the trashcan. It missed. He smiled ruefully.

Lew pulled out his Zippo and fired his cigarette. He walked back around the bed and knelt, picking the package up from where it had fallen. He sat back down on the bed. What in the hell was he going to do?

Obviously he was being watched, had been since the night before. He wondered about the voice on the other end of the line. He shivered at the memory. He looked down at the package, weighing it in his hands. He had an idea, probably a foolish one, but one that would honor Sarah's last request.

Lew slipped his jacket on and put the package back in the pocket and then headed down stairs to the hotel gift shop. After spending some time there, he walked out to get a shoeshine from a Cuban boy in front of the hotel. After that, he returned to his room.

Lew opened a small bottle of whiskey and poured it into one of the plastic cups that the hotel provided. When it reached two fingers in depth and stopped pouring and capped the bottle. He had hoped to hit the big game tonight. Lots of high rollers were going to be there.

Looked like now maybe it wouldn't happen. He took a

sip from the glass, then added ice to it. He had bought a fresh pack of Camels while he was down stairs. He opened it and shook one free after removing his jacket and hanging it in the closet. One side hung down. The weight of the package.

Lew lit his cigarette and wondered about Sarah. Who was she? Why had she been sitting alone in the bar? All he had done was buy her a drink, and he was fairly certain he hadn't been the only one to do so. But she had signaled out him to pass the package too. Why was that?

Lew inhaled, listening to the fire burn the tobacco and the paper tube that surrounded it. He exhaled and took another sip of the whiskey. He wondered about that. What was it about him that had drawn her to him?

Lew hadn't even known he was coming here until he had seen the ad on-line about the big game. Had that ad been a plant? Had somebody known it would draw him in? That was too much to hope for. How could they have known that he would come? Was his bad luck being manufactured?

Lew took another sip of whiskey. His last chance. Had it been a set-up? A last chance at the end of the road. Something that somebody had known would appeal to him.

Lew threw back the rest of the contents of the glass. He sat it down on the nightstand and headed for the door. The jacket remained in the closet, hanging lopsided. The lock clicked shut behind him.

Lew found a small game at the Smoking Tuna and bought into it. He killed a couple of hours and ended two thousand dollars ahead. Yes, his luck was turning. Lew went back to his room.

His jacket was still there, and it was still lopsided on the hanger. It surprised him that the room hadn't been searched. It was something that he would have done. Lew glanced at his watch. Sunset was less than half an hour away. He pulled the jacket on and headed for Mallory Square.

The square was packed with people hoping to see the fabled green flash, rumored to bring good luck to those who saw it. The Green Flash, not a comic book character, but an atmospheric event - that startling glint of neon green that appears just for a second on the upper curve of the sun just as its last little sliver dips under the horizon. An optical sunrise or sunset atmospheric phenomenon, it lasts but a second or two and is the piéce de résistance of an ethereal event, if you are lucky enough to see it. So elusive and mystical, it's the stuff of movies and books.

Lew had no real belief in that particular superstition. People made their own luck. Many gamblers were superstitious, but Lew was not one of them. No, the cards were something easily manipulated, just like most people. The problem he was facing in this particular game was that he didn't know who he was playing against and had not had the chance to learn their tells.

Lew scanned the crowd with his eyes, trying to pick out anyone who might have a particular interest in him. His sunglasses hid his eyes and gave him a chance to look around without looking like that was what he was doing. That's when he spotted them. Two men moving through the crowd almost like guided missiles. Lew puffed on his cigarette and looked around. He saw a familiar face close by. Detective Alvarez. Lew pushed his way through the crowd. He tapped the cop on the shoulder. Alvarez turned around.

"Detective, so good to see you. Have you found out anything more about that poor girl?" Lew asked.

"Mr. Carroll?" Alvarez looked surprised.

"I saw you and wanted to ask," Lew shrugged. Lew maneuvered around so that the detective was between him and the two approaching torpedoes. One of the men frowned and they slipped into a holding pattern amid the throng of oohing and awing tourists. He knew the sun was sinking closer to the horizon behind him.

"I appreciate your asking, but no, so far we don't have anymore information," Alvarez shrugged. Lew picked that moment to slip the thin package into the cop's jacket pocket.

"She seemed like a really nice girl. I hate what happened to her," Lew told him. Alvarez nodded and Lew turned and walked away. He was pretty sure that the two torpedoes were tracking him again. He allowed himself a smile as he worked his way to the rail. He flipped his cigarette to the ground and crushed it under his shoe.

Suddenly the two men were on either side of him. "Mr. Carroll, will you come with us please?" one asked politely.

"But what if I miss the green flash? I was hoping to change my luck?" Lew said nonchalantly.

"No optical illusion is gonna help you, Pal," the other man said as he grabbed Lew's arm hard, his thick blunt fingers digging painfully into muscle. Lew half-turned, driving his hand into the man's throat, the webbing between his thumb and forefinger smashing his Adam's apple crushing the hyoid bone and his larynx, causing him to start choking on his blood. Lew spun, his fist shooting out and cracking the other man on the jaw and dropping him. Lew slipped off into the crowd, leaving the two men behind him.

People started shouting as he walked away, but most of them didn't notice him. Lew headed for a piano bar called The Keys. There was a jazz quartet playing there when he entered. Lew walked to the bar and ordered whiskey. The bartender poured him two fingers of single malt scotch and Marlow slipped him a c-note. "Any games going?" he asked. The bartender looked him over and nodded towards a door near the back of the bar. Lew nodded back and took his drink with him.

The room was dingy and smoke filled. Four men sat around the table. Lew recognized three of them. There was an open chair and he dropped into it. Lew tossed a thousand dollars on the table. One of the other men pushed a stack of chips at him and the money disappeared from the table. Lew dug out a cigarette and lit it as the cards were dealt.

It was dark when Lew Carroll left the bar and the game. He was up $5,000.00 from when he had arrived on Key West. He had thought about hailing a cab when he left the bar, but had then decided not to endanger anyone else. Whoever had sent those guys to Mallory Square was playing for keeps. Lew decided he didn't want to get any innocents involved. He walked towards his hotel.

The door to his room was partially open when he reached it. Lew stood outside, wondering about going in. He couldn't hear anything from inside. Lew pushed the door open and stepped inside. He hit the light switch and checked the room. It was empty, but it had very obviously been searched.

Of course he had known it would be. He figured whoever was after the package might think it was in his room. He shut the door behind him and had begun straightening up the room when the phone started the ring. Lew let it ring as he gathered his things and put them back on hangers and into drawers. The phone stopped for several minutes and then started to ring again. This time he answered it.

"Hello?" he said.

"I'm not happy, Mr. Carroll," the deep sepulchral voice announced.

"I'm really not sure I give a fuck. You tried to set me up for a fucking hit," Lew replied as he fished out a cigarette and lit it. He knew that the other man could hear the cigarette burning through the phone.

"You have my property, Mr. Carroll. I will get it back."

"What's to say I haven't already given it to the cops? There was a detective in Mallory Square tonight," Lew replied, blowing smoke rings towards the ceiling.

"Are you saying that's what happened?" the voice asked.

"I'm saying nothing. But you want what I have, I want compensated."

"Compensated how?"

"Cash. Untraceable small bills."

"It would be so much simpler just to kill you."

"But then you might not get what you want. Are you willing to risk that?" Lew asked, smiling.

"How much?" the voice asked wearily.

"One hundred thousand dollars," Lew told him.

"Outrageous!" snapped the voice on the other end of the line.

"Have it your way," Lew broke the connection and sat there waiting. He didn't have to wait long. The phone was ringing within thirty seconds. Lew answered it.

"When and where?" the voice asked.

"Harpoon Harry's about 10:00am," Lew told him.

"See you then," the voice replied and the connection was broken.

Everything was in place. Lew dialed the Key West police station. He asked for Sgt. Alvarez.

"Alvarez," a familiar voice said.

"Did you get the package I left in your coat?" Lew asked, exhaling more smoke.

"I did. That was a slick piece of work. You responsible for those two guys in Mallory Square?" Alvarez asked.

"You want the guy that killed the girl?" Lew asked.

"You know I do," Alvarez replied.

"Be at Harpoon Harry's in the morning at ten o'clock," Lew told him. He broke the connection and after locking his door, stripped down to his skivvies and slept like a baby.

Lew Carroll was up with the sun. He took a long shower and dressed and then went downstairs for some coffee. He killed time by reading both the Citizen and the Miami Herald before walking over to Harpoon Harry's. Ron greeted him as he entered and Lew ordered a *café con leche* as he perused the menu.

At five till ten, a large black man entered the bar, a small package under his arm. Lew had already spotted Detective Alvarez a few tables away. The cop ignored him and Lew was fine with that. The black man slid into the seat across from Lew.

"Mr. Carroll," the man said.

"You are?" Lew asked. The man looked very uncomfortable.

"Jonas Griffin," the man replied.

"Nice to finally meet you, Jonas. You say Sarah had something that belonged to you. What exactly would that be?" Lew asked.

"None of your business, Mr. Carroll," Jonas replied.

"Wrong. It became my business when you murdered Sarah," Lew told him.

"Are you a sentimentalist?" Jonas asked.

"More of a romantic," Lew shrugged.

"You had feelings for the girl? Someone you met only once?"

"Love at first sight, what can I say?" Lew shrugged. He stubbed his cigarette out in the crystal ashtray.

"I'm going to kill you, Mr. Carroll," Jonas said softly.

"No, you're not," Lew replied.

"Why is that?" Jonas asked. Lew pulled out his cigarettes and shook one free. He tucked the unfiltered Camel into the corner of his mouth and put the pack back in his pocket before fishing out his battered silver Zippo. Lew rolled the striker wheel under his thumb and a burst of blue-yellow flame appeared. He touched the end of the paper tube to it, drawing the flame up through it. Lew clicked the lighter closed and looked at the man across the table from him.

"Because you're under arrest for the murder of Sarah Clark," Lew smiled. Sgt. Alvarez came up behind Jonas, snatching his arm up and slapping a cuff first on one wrist and then the other. He began reading the man his rights. Lew Carroll smiled. Alvarez hadn't bothered the package that Jonas had carried in. Lew made it disappear in his pocket.

Sarah had been a reporter investigating the drug trade and corruption on Key West. Carol Doyle was her editor. Lew had copied the information and gave it to the police after sending a copy to the Miami Herald and knowing that the Key West police knew it. Lew Carroll lit another cigarette and watched as the police dragged Jonas away...

4.
DISTURBANCE IN THE FIELD

Lucy Burdette

The blood had soaked into each nubby crevice of the white carpet, leaving the loops standing at attention, stiff with dried brown. I grimaced. It would be hell to remove the stain.

Over the past few years, I've been unlucky enough to witness the aftermath of several murders. And good gravy, I'm a food critic, not a cop. So I've learned how my mind handles physical trauma and the ensuing gore: I focus on housekeeping details. Not that I'm a clean freak, but thinking about cleansers and enzymes keeps me from puking on the crime scene.

Detective Bransford gestured toward the stain. "Apparently the vic was whacked here."

Vic, perp, floater, whack – Bransford and his buddies handle trauma with cop language, a not-so-secret code that tries to blur the hard truth: A woman died here.

"Her husband called 911 about four hours ago," Bransford continued. "Told us he'd been in the shower. Thought he maybe heard a banging or popping noise, maybe he didn't. The window was open, which the husband says isn't status quo." He waved at the fluttering chintz, then steered me around the stain and out into the hall.

"Don't touch anything."

I rolled my eyes. "Duh."

"I posted an officer in the kitchen with Mr. Harrison after our interview this morning. There's a neighbor waiting with him too." Bransford's brows arched, thicker and darker than the burr of brown hair on his head.

"Did she arrive with a casserole?" I asked. "They say single women have gotten aggressive these days." I'm single but Bransford isn't, not exactly. And I'm not at all – aggressive, that is.

He grinned. "Nah, I kind of suggested she hang around to hold his hand. He acted all broken up when they came for the body."

"Acted?" I still couldn't quite figure out why he'd allowed me to ride along on this case on our way to lunch. Usually he's busy telling me to stay out of police business, but this time he seemed to want my opinion. I pulled my elbow from his grip. "What direction are we facing?"

"I don't know. North? Northwest? What the hell difference does that make?"

I tapped a finger on my lower lip. "So wait. The woman was found here?"

"Oddly enough," Bransford's Adam's apple dropped an inch, then bobbed back into place, "after she was shot, she appears to have pulled herself down this hall, across the vestibule, and into their bedroom." His eyes darted away then back to my face. "I'll show you."

We traced the path the injured woman had taken, hugging the walls to avoid contaminating the blood smears that marked the victim's travel. A small crew of crime scene technicians was packing up after a morning scraping samples and spreading fingerprint dust. The chi-chi décor would never be the same.

"So her husband found her in the bedroom when he

got out of the shower?" I asked.

"No. He was using the facilities in the guest room on the far side of the house." Bransford's eyebrows peaked a second time. "Then he claims he came to the master to get fresh clothes and voila – found his dead wife. Look around for a minute, then come on down to the kitchen. Don't touch anything," he said again.

When Bransford told me we were stopping here on the way to lunch, he said they needed a female perspective. Someone familiar with a little woo-woo, he'd added, with scorn in his voice. Friendship with a Key West tarot card reader qualified me.

I moved around the perimeter of the room, building a mental picture of the woman who had lived here. And died here too. Only later, at home, over a glass of wine on the houseboat, would I allow myself to think about that final gruesome drag.

A king-sized bed draped with a hand-stitched gold quilt dominated the room. I'd seen the same coverlet in a high-end bedding catalog last month. Unless the woman had lucked out in a major January white sale, the quilt cost almost my weekly income as the living and food editor at *Key Zest* magazine.

Half a dozen pillows had been plumped at the head of the bed. A person reclining here would have a primo view of the backyard garden. Orchids, bromeliads, schefflera, and some plants I didn't recognize – they all pinwheeled out from the marble torso of a nude and muscular man that had been positioned next to a dipping pool. The ground around the plantings had been freshly buried under dark mulch. A hundred yards or so behind the garden stretched the Atlantic Ocean.

I studied the second, smaller bloodstain on the carpet beside the bed. Why would a woman with a lethal injury drag herself the length of the house to her bedroom to call for help? Surely in a home that bordered on opulent, there would have been a closer phone. Maybe she realized that her husband was busy elsewhere and would never hear her cries. Or maybe there was no point in looking for a savior in the man who'd shot you. I folded the underside of the quilt back, knelt down, and peered under the bed – nothing out of place except for a stub of red cord protruding between the mattress and box spring.

I poked my head into the master bath – a large whirlpool tub, his and hers sinks – blue pottery bowls set into white limestone, a separate shower big enough for two, even a bidet. With a bathroom like this, why would Mr. Harrison have showered in the guest quarters?

His and hers walk-in closets were immaculate. The dead woman's clothing hung on padded hangers, arranged by color. A bright red silk blouse launched a sweeping U-turn that ended with a pair of white linen pants. Above the clothes were rows of handbags and matching shoes – no tangle of red high-tops and sequined flip-flops like you'd find in my closet. This was not a woman who would have left a bloodstain the entire length of her carpeted hallway without a darn good reason.

I stepped back out into the bedroom and walked to the gleaming cherry wood bureau. A black scarf had been draped over the mirror, flanked by two delicate ceramic swans. The couple's wedding photo was propped in the middle of the polished surface. I leaned in for a closer look. They appeared happy – though most couples manage that in front of a wedding photographer. She had been a petite woman with black curls and elfin dimples. Mr. Harrison's smile was more reserved. Wide shoulders strained at the seams of his tuxedo.

I left the room to join the detective in the kitchen with the new widower.

"Mr. Harrison, I'm so sorry for your loss." I laid a

quick, comforting hand on his shoulder and noticed that the muscular hunk from the wedding picture had grown rounded and soft.

"Gary," he said.

"This is Ms. Snow," Detective Bransford said tersely. "She's – " He cleared his throat. "She's on my team."

Not technically true, but how else could he explain that he'd brought a food critic to a crime scene? Besides, he looked crabby and grim. So I let it slide.

"Mr. Harrison and I were reviewing the list of suspects we developed this morning," Bransford said, emphasizing *list* and *developed*. He tapped a small, yellow-lined pad on the table, causing a water glass filled with a jumble of white roses to tremble.

"Pilates instructor" were the only words on it.

"Was your wife having a problem with her exercise teacher?" I asked politely.

Mr. Harrison's face caved. "I think, no, I'm almost sure she was having an affair." He ran his hands through his thinning hair, which stuck out in disordered tufts, as though he'd forgotten to comb it once he'd gotten out of the shower. Finding your wife murdered would render the finer points of grooming obsolete.

"What were the signs of that?" Bransford asked.

"She was paying a lot of attention to her dress and her hair," he reported, then pinched the bridge of his nose with his fingers. "And our neighbor told me she saw him over here all the time."

"Your wife was generally sloppy?" I asked. This did not fit with what I'd seen in the bedroom.

"Not sloppy exactly. You know how it is when you've been married a while. You just don't take the same care you did when you were dating."

"Those early courtship days are special times," I said with a warm smile.

Bransford snorted softly and put a finger to his lips: He wanted me to shut up.

I ignored him. "How often did the trainer come?"

"I paid for twice a week." Mr. Harrison scowled. "Our neighbor thinks he was throwing in freebies."

"So your wife was taking care of herself that way," said Bransford.

"Very good care," grunted Mr. Harrison.

"Did you ever run into this man outside of their sessions?"

He shook his head. "Never met the jerk."

"Wasn't your neighbor here earlier?" I asked.

"I sent her home," said Bransford, frowning furiously. Then he turned to Mr. Harrison. "Let's go over your morning again."

"I had an early business meeting – a couple of sets of tennis over at Bayview Park and breakfast at Harpoon Harry's with one of my customers," Mr. Harrison explained. "I forgot to bring pants to change for the office so I figured I'd come home to shower and go to work from here."

"Why shower in the guest room?" asked Bransford.

Mr. Harrison twisted his hands and shrugged. "No reason, really."

"Have you and your wife been experiencing marital difficulties?" Bransford asked.

"No! Dammit, I didn't kill my own wife." His fist crashed down onto the kitchen table. A smattering of rose petals fluttered to the table and tears filled his eyes.

I leaned forward and touched his hand. "Your home is so lovely. I don't seem to have the accessories gene. Was your wife interested in decorating or did she hire someone for that kind of thing?"

"She did it herself. In fact, she just finished redoing the bedroom. Which looked fine before she went and tore it all out, thank you very much. We had a hell of a fight over that one. You can't imagine the charge card bills the past few months." Seeming to realize what he'd said, he grimaced and dragged a hand over his eyes. "I don't mean a knock-down, drag-out," he said, "I just complained about the American Express, that's all."

"And did she enjoy gardening?"

"She designed all that, too. But she hired some Hispanics to help with the heavy lifting." He fitted his hand to his lumbar spine. "I have a bad back."

Detective Bransford stood up. "Thank you for your cooperation, Mr. Harrison. Please stick around. I'll want to touch base with you later on. Meantime, call me if you think of anything else that might be helpful." He scribbled down his cell phone number and handed over the card.

We left the house and paused on the front porch. Veranda was more like it. I inhaled a double lungful of salt air and tilted my face up to the sun.

"Were you going to ask him for his wife's recipe collection next?" said Bransford.

"Just wanted to get a picture of her life here." I turned to him and smiled. "Isn't that why you asked me along?"

He didn't answer. Then: "What the hell is Pilates anyway?"

"You need to get out more often, Detective. Everybody's doing Pilates now. It's about strengthening your core abdominal and back muscles. And lengthening your spine – even men get osteoporosis. You should try it."

He grunted, but straightened his shoulders. He had six-pack abs from what I'd noticed, but probably earned in the gym, the old-fashioned way with crunches and planks.

"What did you think?" I asked. "Mr. Harrison seemed genuinely upset to me. They may have had some problems, but I get the feeling that he really loved her."

Bransford rolled his eyes. "I like him for it. He shot her

and then took a shower to eliminate any physical evidence. Guy who's loaded like that, gonna cost a fortune to legally dump a wife he's tired of. He's upset, sure he is – who'd want to trade this mansion for a cellblock?"

"But?" I asked.

"But something stinks," he admitted. "We may need a rain check on lunch. I have to chat with the neighbor, then head into town and check out the trainer. Michelson will pick him up at the studio and bring him to the station."

"I'll tag along," I said.

We crossed a carefully tended expanse of pachysandra, my feet sinking into the soft sand underneath the vegetation with each step. Two enormous marble lions guarded the front door of this hacienda-style home. The face of the lion on the left had been broken off, leaving just the mane and the enormous paws. The choppy waves of the ocean glinted in the distance. Not quite the view the Harrisons had, but stunning all the same.

A worried-looking woman with white-blond hair opened the door before Bransford's finger made contact with the bell. The heavy layer of eyeliner below her left eye had blurred as though she'd been crying. Hard. Her voice was shaky.

"Thank God you're on the case, Detective. I feel so frightened. I can't believe this is happening. I saw Vivian in the garden just this morning."

"May we sit down a minute?" He didn't bother to introduce me this time.

"I'm Liza Renquist." The woman perched her moist hand on my wrist briefly, then turned toward the living room. Everything in the room was white.

"Take your shoes off," I hissed, but Bransford just glared. I stepped out of my flip-flops, leaving them on a mat next to a pair of silver sandals and some pruning shears.

"Sorry for the mess." Mrs. Renquist waved at a few scattered shreds of mulch that definitely wouldn't qualify as a "mess" in most homes. "I was working in the yard when Gary ran over with this awful news." She began to weep and sank into the couch.

I brushed off the seat of my pants before sitting – just my luck to transfer some glop from Bransford's unmarked to this woman's pristine upholstery.

"Take me through what happened this morning, all the details you can remember," Bransford told her.

"There's nothing to tell, really. I didn't hear anything. Like I said, I waved at Vivian from my garden. I like to do my work early" – she patted her cheek and glanced at me – "sun damage, you know? Though you're too young to worry about that. Anyway, Vivian seemed just fine. Then a couple hours ago, Gary ran over and – " her voice broke – "told me Vivian had been shot." She crossed her arms over her chest and clutched her thin shoulders with both hands. "I don't know how I'll ever sleep tonight – my husband's on the road until Friday."

"Did you notice anything unusual in the Casa Marina neighborhood this morning, Mrs. Renquist?" asked Bransford. "Cars you didn't recognize? Visitors? Anything like that?"

"We do get people biking by, and rarely, the homeless…" She shook her head. "Well, I was a little surprised to see her in exercise clothes so early."

Bransford blinked. "Vivian?"

Mrs. Renquist nodded slowly.

"What do you know about the Harrisons' marriage?" he asked. "Don't hold back, Mrs. Renquist. We need to know the honest truth."

"Honestly? I don't think they've been getting along." She wiped her eyes, angled her head toward her neighbor's estate, and dropped her voice to a whisper. "I'm pretty sure she was doing it with the Pilates instructor." A small smile played across her lips. "He *is* a very nice looking man. Middle-aged husbands tend to get a little flabby." Her gaze raked the detective's torso. He pulled back his shoulders and sucked in his gut. Then she looked at me again and smiled.

"Be sure and lock your doors, Ma'am, and call us if you notice anything out of the ordinary." Bransford placed his card on the coffee table and got to his feet. "I may need to talk with you again."

"Any time. Can I get you some tea or a sandwich? Oh my goodness, my manners have gone all to heck." She began to cry again.

"Thanks, no."

"Your roses are stunning," I said, motioning to a crystal vase filled with white buds.

"Thanks," she snuffled.

I slipped back into my shoes and followed Bransford out the door and across the lawn.

"Whaddya think?" he asked, pausing just outside the Harrison mansion.

"The honest truth?" I teased. "Interviewing the Pilates instructor will be a waste of time. May we go back inside the other house?"

Bransford looked at his iPhone, then gave a curt nod. "Make it fast. What did you think you saw?"

I led Bransford down the hallway to the bedroom and pointed to the wedding photo displayed on the cherry bureau and then a smaller headshot of the bridal couple on the bedside table. "I believe Vivian was looking for this picture when she made that trip along the hall."

"Of course," said Bransford, knocking the heel of his hand against his forehead. "She was going to implicate her husband by marking his likeness with her blood." He snorted. "You're losing it. Why didn't she just call the cops and tell us straight out?"

"May I?" I gestured to the phone. He nodded, and I plucked it from the receiver, pressed "call", and handed it over to him. "No dial tone."

Bransford squatted and ran his hand along the cord until he discovered a cut in the line. He looked annoyed. One of his men should have picked this up.

"She probably tried to call you. Then, knowing she was dying, she left a clue."

"A clue," he said flatly. His knees cracked as he stood.

I pushed on. "This is the room of a woman who's committed to working on her marriage. I do not believe she was having an affair with the Pilates instructor. She was using the principles of Feng Shui to put her relationship with her husband back together. I think it was starting to work, too. You saw how grief-stricken he was."

"Fung schway?" said Bransford. "What the hell?"

"It's the ancient Chinese art of placement to allow optimal movement of chi or natural energy in your home." I folded the golden quilt back away from the sheets and knelt to touch the end of the red cord sandwiched between the box spring and the mattress. "The rope represents a loving tie."

"So now you want me to solve murders according to some Oriental fruitcake philosophy?" The detective's voice brimmed with disgust.

"Asian. Asian is for people, Oriental for carpets." I smiled and got back to my feet. "It's not just the rope," I added. "The signs are everywhere – the wedding photos, the sensuous bedspread, the colorful garden, even the swan statues. If you're working on a stronger marriage, they suggest you decorate with pairs of animals that mate for life."

Bransford scowled. "Where in the name of Christ do you get this stuff?"

"And the cloth over the mirror," I added. "She covered it because a mirror facing a bed invites failure in the marriage due to infidelity with a third party." I tucked a strand of hair behind my ear and stared at the point just below his Adam's apple. He'd loosened his tie just enough to expose a sprig of hair. "May I make a suggestion?"

"Since when do you ask permission?"

I smiled sweetly. "Find out whether the Harrisons made love today. If so, and if I was a cop, I'd check Mrs. Renquist's hands for gunshot residue. Here's my theory: she came over to share some roses and saw more than she bargained for – the Harrisons having sex. Gary was the one having the affair, not Vivian. And the affair was with Liza Renquist herself. She saw them having marital relations, was overcome with jealousy, dumped the roses, and marched back over with a gun to confront Vivian once Gary left for work. You saw the outcome."

Bransford tipped his head toward one shoulder, then the other. "And you based this theory on home decorating?"

"And the mulch on her sandals. The mulch in the Renquist garden is red, not black. And the roses on Mr. Harrison's kitchen table. Did you notice? They came from Mrs. Renquist's garden." I pointed out the window to the neighbor's bushy white flowers. "Mrs. Harrison chose plants that are colorful and native to south Florida – nothing manicured and nothing white."

Forty-five minutes later, we watched two uniformed cops lead the handcuffed Liza Renquist down the front walk to a waiting patrol car. She was growling like a nasty little dog.

"Solving murders through Fung Schway," said Bransford. "What a crock. How the hell do I explain this one to the chief?"

"Did the job, right? You go ahead and explain it however you like," I said graciously. "But I would like to hear why you really brought me along."

Bransford sighed. "I thought you'd find something in the casseroles. I thought you might apply some of that culinary expertise I'm always hearing about while I interviewed Harrison."

"I don't think so." I waggled my finger. "You felt the disturbance in the energy field as soon as you entered the living room – same as I did. And you remembered, subconsciously perhaps, the discussion we had last week about my Feng Shui consultation."

"Baloney. Wait a minute, though." Bransford placed two fingers from each hand on his forehead. "I'm receiving a message now. Wait...wait...it's about Kung Pao."

He massaged his temples. "Kung Pao chicken to be exact. And a Tsingtao beer. Shall we take out or eat in?"

5.
THE WALLS HAD EARS
Murder at 2929

Ben Harrison

umidity mixed with the heat rising from the blacktop caused their clothes to stick to their bodies as they taxied toward the end of the runway. In order to get more air circulating in the cockpit, Frank Henley partially opened the small hatch he used to get in and out of the plane when cargo blocked the larger cabin door in the rear.

Lisa, sitting on the fold-down seat between the pilots' seats, and Matt, in the co-pilot's chair, were both looking out at the ocean paralleling the airstrip at the airport just east of Coxen's Hole, Roatán, Honduras. One of several islands located about ninety miles from the mainland of Honduras, it is surrounded by one of the most beautiful coral reefs in the world. For Henley Air Freight, the trip had been a routine delivery of refrigeration parts. For Matt, a barroom singer, and Lisa, a recently divorced cocktail waitress, it had been a much needed mini-vacation after dealing with the throngs of people visiting during the Christmas/New Year's week back in Key West.

In the cockpit, sweating enough to spot his shirt, Frank pressed the right brake and revved the left engine causing the tail of the silver Beechcraft D-18 to semi-circle around into the wind. Brakes set, the plane shook with eagerness when he ran up the right and then the left Pratt and Whitney nine-cylinder rotary engine as he went through the checklist and scanned the horizon for incoming aircraft. There was no control tower.

Frank, with practiced expertise, closed the hatch and moved the throttles full forward. The tail lifted almost immediately. Even after the thousands of hours Frank had flown, it was still exciting to feel the exact moment when the rubber left the ground – landing gear up – throttle back some – bank to the north over the hills of Roatán that were not quite large enough to be called mountains. Warm updrafts from the ground below created a turbulence that bounced the plane occasionally as they passed over Anthony's Cay Resort and Half Moon Bay. The water viewed from the air, was a spectacular panorama of indigo, turquoise, yellows and blues. The air cooled dramatically as they ascended.

"We should be able to see the west end of Cuba and

the Isle of Pines before the weather gets rough," Frank said over the engine noise, which was still loud but quieter now that they were at altitude. "I don't think it will be choppy long, only when we go through the leading edge of the cold front."

It was an older airplane, and Lisa, Matt and Frank had to talk in voices above normal discussing the things that had to be done to make the run-down house the three of them had just bought in Key West livable. They would be moving in at the end of the month, which was only a week away. Rather than pay rent, financially it had made sense for them to invest their combined resources for the down payment on 2929 Virginia Street, across from Bayview Park. Well aware that there was a lot of cleaning and fixing up that had to be done, at least the improvements would be going into something they owned.

Matt, who had done just about every job in the books to afford his musical habit, knew the most about home construction, but Frank, a good mechanic, wasn't far behind. Lisa didn't know how to do much practical except look exceptionally good, yet she was ready for anything that didn't resemble her former life. The mildewed, waterlogged, fake tile surrounding the bathtub would have to be ripped out and replaced with cement board before it could be re-tiled. The wood below the peeling linoleum floor was soft so they'd have to deal with whatever they found underneath before laying the Mexican terra cotta tile Lisa had chosen. Thankfully, the refrigerator and stove worked.

The discussion trailed off as they closed in on the black clouds that kept appearing larger as they neared a cold front that was on its way south. Flying over the Straits between Cuba and México, the lights of Cozumél were barely visible off to their left. The water below was changing from the startling white-capped blue of the afternoon to the ominous dark of evening while the sun silhouetted enormous billowing cumulonimbus thunderheads.

"God, this is exciting, Frank. Is it always this awesome in a huge way?" Lisa had been waitressing at Lou's for over a year now, and the barroom lingo had crept into her vocabulary. It was hard to keep it out.

"I see why you love it the way you do. I mean, sitting in the passenger section of a commercial jet you look out of the window and see the clouds but it's nothing like this. We are so tiny and those clouds are monstrous." Lisa was right; that was one of the reasons Frank loved flying. Really flying that is, with twin piston engines rattling the forty-five-year-old Beechcraft through the air. That some D-18's were still flying was fairly remarkable. They had, against all odds, remained competitive because they could carry heavy loads.

It was getting cool enough that Frank put on some cabin heat just before the rain began pelting the windshield. You could hear it hitting the plane's aluminum skin as it flew at 150 knots per hour, the sound layered beneath the engine noise. The drops would hit and then turn into tiny straight streams across the windshield as the speed of the airplane blew the water backwards. The twinge of fear she felt was the exhilarating kind. It was dangerously beautiful, skirting dark thunderheads with an occasional ray of sunshine piercing the rain and the clouds.

Suddenly, Frank began mouthing obscenities and reacting to a red warning light that buzzed and blinked on the instrument panel. He grabbed the left engine throttle and pulled it back as fast as he could, the needle of the oil pressure gauge rapidly moving from green to the red danger area.

Immediately, he shut it down and took a look at the

failed engine's cowling using his flashlight. Oil was running down the cover.

"I'm sure as hell glad this happened on the way home, when the plane's empty. It looks like we're gonna see how this old lady flies on one engine. We're holding altitude," he said several minutes later.

The glow of the instrument panel and outside running lights faintly illuminated the cockpit and the clouds they were flying through.

Less than a hundred miles from Key West, Frank had his headset on and was talking into the handheld microphone.

"Key West International, this is Henley Air Freight, twin Beech, 7327 Echo. Do you read? Over."

"Roger 7327 Echo. Loud and clear, Frank. Over."

"Key West, we're about seventy miles southeast at an altitude of 9,500 feet on a course of five-zero degrees. I've lost an engine. I don't see any problem reaching the field or maintaining altitude, but I think one pass is all we get. How's the weather there? Please advise. Over."

"Roger, 7327 Echo, ceiling 2,000 feet, visibility 3 miles, wind out of the north gusting to 35 knots, we have you on radar. Standby. Over."

The tone of the control tower changed quickly from friendly to business because, even though the airport was open, the weather was foul. It was the air controller's job to clear the runway and prepare for an emergency landing. The fire trucks and ambulances had to be in place.

Every time the plane hit an air pocket their hearts picked up a beat. Frank glanced at Lisa and patted her on the knee, "We're going to make it. Sorry our first trip is turning out to be so thrilling."

She smiled at him, aware that she was enjoying the drama and tension enormously. Landing the Beechcraft was second nature to him, he'd done it thousands of times

... on two engines. With one engine, it was highly doubtful the plane would be able to re-gain altitude if he came in too low or overshot the narrow, short landing strip that runs west to east. When there's a strong crosswind, it's always tricky.

"7327 Echo, you are cleared to land."

Slowly descending through the soup, Frank had been flying on instruments for what seemed like a long time. As they bounced one way then the other, the plane, not far from Ft. Zachary Taylor, finally emerged from the cloud cover. Suddenly, the headlights and whirling emergency lights of the fire engines and two ambulances reflected off of the wet taxiway next to the runway. Should they crash, there would be a mad scramble by the firefighters to soak the plane with foam and, in fire retardant suits, attempt to rescue those inside.

It was up to Frank to visually determine the flight path.

Gear down, landing lights on, the flight tactic Frank would use is called "slipping." Using the ailerons as though making a slight turn to windward and crossing them with the rudder, the aircraft literally slips into the wind allowing it to line up with the runway. Wanting to keep his airspeed up, he was coming in without flaps.

Just past the red approach lights, over the broad white stripes at the beginning of the landing surface, it seemed as though the left wing might hit the ground as the plane bucked randomly, but throttling back, pulling the yoke of the wheel back to pull the nose up, coming in a little hot, the left and then the right tire skidded slightly before grabbing the rain slicked concrete. Tail wheel down, there was plenty of room to apply the brakes and slow the aircraft before the end of the runway.

Matt and Lisa, white-knuckling the armrests, exhaled and started releasing their grip. Frank, sounding routine, made contact with the tower as he maneuvered the twin Beech toward the exit ramp.

In a deadpan voice, the tower congratulated him on the landing and gave him permission to clear the runway and taxi to the tarmac several hundred feet ahead, near the Federal Express office. Now that they were safely on the ground, the airport could be re-opened.

As he lowered the rear fuselage door, Frank grinned and started whistling the theme song from the movie, *The High and the Mighty*, the way John Wayne did after he lost a couple of engines and had to coax his passenger filled DC-6 home.

It was probably a blown gasket – relatively easy to repair. Henley Air Freight and its sole proprietor, Frank Henley, would fly again, probably the day after tomorrow assuming the problem was what he thought it was and there were no parts hassles.

Leaning over underneath the wings, he put chocks on the wheels and tied the plane down as Lisa and Matt unloaded their gear. Without cargo, Frank was able to clear customs over the phone. The paperwork required when there is an emergency landing could be filled out the next day.

"I'll drive, you've done enough. Let's go to my place," she said. "Might as well enjoy the luxury while we can." Walking in the cold steady rain from the plane to Frank's beat-up old Plymouth Volaré station wagon, she was indeed a sight to behold. Without an umbrella, wearing a soft, white blouse without a brassiere, her exquisitely rounded breasts, could be seen clearly through the wet material. Feeling very much alive, she really didn't care.

"That was incredible." Lisa's dark eyes seemed to glow. "The way you took her in like that."

"Impressive. It's good to be here," Matt added in his wry, understated way. "I was reading a John D. McDonald book the other day, and he was talking about how good it felt to be shot at and missed."

Moving-day from their respective apartments using a rented U-Haul was long and hard. The matrasses, box springs and bed frames along with suitcases filled with clothes had to be carried upstairs to their individual bedrooms. The rest of their combined possessions were stacked in the middle of the living room so they could do the work the downstairs needed.

Had there not been a woman involved, the effort Frank and Matt put into improving their new home would have been considerably less. Trying to please Lisa, whom they were both in love with – everyone who saw her was – took more effort. Part of the deal – set in stone – was: don't even think about trying to fuck me. She'd had enough "love" for a while. Her former husband and her former life had somehow not been enough, and she was still slightly confused as to why she had made some radical decisions.

Matt was tall and lanky with a bushy mustache. Frank, slightly shorter, was clean-shaven with a boyish face and dirty blond hair. Lisa, well Lisa was someone who wandered through life with a built-in advantage. Italian perfection that could physically take a person's breath away, she may have acted as though she didn't have an effect on men, but she knew she did, and that it could be severe. Unfortunately, all she wanted was a little room to breathe without the responsibilities of a romantic relationship. Moving to Key West, far from her home in San Francisco, symbolized her resolve to begin again on her own.

Leaving her familiar surroundings had been difficult and, deep down, it hurt leaving the man she had married "until death us do part" much more than she thought it would. She missed him in bed at night. She missed him in the morning before breakfast, before he put on his suit and tie and headed for the office.

"Why'd you leave him?" Matt asked as he sat on the side of the bathtub putting yellow tile on the cement drywall he bought at Strunk Lumber. Yellow was the only color that would go well with the avocado colored bathtub and toilet.

"I'm still asking myself that question, and there isn't any real reason. My parents are completely baffled and think I've gone off the deep end. Maybe I have.

"I didn't catch him with his secretary. He didn't beat me. I'd have to say he materially gave me everything a normal wife could ask for." Lisa was on a ladder painting her bedroom a pale, lime green. The air from another cold front, like the one that had given them their brush with mortality, had created a day that simply couldn't be any more perfect – clear blue skies, temperature in the mid to upper seventies. Through the open jalousie windows, Lisa could see brilliant red bougainvillea framed by lush green foliage.

"Well?" Matt said waiting for some kind of reply. His view from the bathtub was decidedly worse, and the Thinset adhesive he was applying to the tiles was beginning to spread all over everything.

"I don't know."

"That clears things up. You're probably going to leave us and go back to him after I've put up all these tiles you insisted on."

She hadn't really talked much about what she had done and the words weren't easy to find. "Maybe things were too pat, too easy, too set. I've always been interested in theatre work, so I guess I could blame Ray for being less than enthusiastic about that. He didn't want me gone at night because nights were the only time we had together. He usually golfed on Sundays.

"I had a part in a play called *Lend Me A Tenor*. It was perfect for me and my Italian looks." Lisa's maiden name was Sabastini, and she came by her dark hair and brown eyes honestly. "I was the tempestuous wife of an Opera star who was always hiding girlfriends in various closets. It was a slapstick comedy. I got to storm around in fancy clothes. It was fun...

"Anyhow, Ray came backstage and found me taking off my makeup in a bra and thong. It was no big deal, the only men around were two gay actors and a sixty-nine-year-old set designer. Ray was livid. I promised, from then on that in male company, I would keep all of my clothes on all of the time, but that wasn't it...

"After the play had run its dates, before our vacation to Key West that made me start questioning things, I bought new clothes – summer clothes – shorts, tops, a new bathing suit. We were staying at the Pier House. Now, for some reason I could sunbathe without my top on at the beach there. Ray actually encouraged it, thought it was European.

"After lunch one afternoon, walking back to the hotel in my matching outfit, it dawned on me that I was going to be a tourist for the rest of my life if things kept going the way they were. Actually, I felt like a tourist in our relationship. We just didn't have much to say to each other as we walked holding hands."

Painting and thinking, her mind went back to the day she had gotten up the nerve to tell him there must be more to life and that she was leaving. Surprised, astounded and angry, he resisted, but eventually there wasn't much he could do about it. She didn't want money.

Frank was a curious one who loved the library. He was constantly trying to talk Matt and Lisa into coming with him to the research room. In fact, he was trying to talk Matt into writing a song about "Bum" Farto. There really had been a fire chief by that name in the sixties. Apparently, he had become involved with the cocaine and marijuana smuggling that was so prevalent in Key West and had been busted. "Mysteriously, Bum, who was known for his trademark red sports coat, drove off in a red rent-a-car with the top rolled down. To this day no one knows where Bum Farto is," Frank relayed to Matt who wasn't sure whether or not Frank was pulling his leg.

"'Bum' Farto, you've got to be kidding. No one has a name like Bum Farto."

"Check it out, Matt. I swear there's a song there."

In the history section, according to old maps Lisa found, their house was the second one built in that part of town. Bayview Park was just a bunch of empty land on the outskirts. El Gato, the big house near where Fausto's Food Palace on White Street would be, was built about the same time. Back then horse-drawn trolleys on steel tracks ran on White and turned around one block over on Varela. When their house was constructed, a two-by-four was actually two inches by four inches, not three-and-a-half by one-and-one-half inches. That's why the structural studs in the bathroom looked so big.

Lisa's curiosity had become piqued after taking Frank up on his invitation to come with him to the Monroe County Library. She soon learned that Tom Hambright, the library historian, was a living encyclopedia.

"It makes you wonder what all has happened in that old house, doesn't it? If only the walls had ears."

Her long black hair fell softly around her shoulders and the white of her teeth showed momentarily as her smile grew and her lips parted. Ramón, putting his arm around her waist, whispered and grinned with confident fearlessness, anticipating another reckless rendezvous. "It won't be long, less than an hour. Go, wait for me at the house, go."

Ramón pulled open the screen door and went back inside the kitchen of Pepe's Cafe on Duval Street, just around the corner from a new bar called Sloppy Joe's on Greene Street, next to the telegraph office. It was eleven o'clock and a yellow quarter moon was just above the slightly run-down shops with paint peeling off of the wooden storefronts.

Eva's leather shoes made a clicking sound on the reddish-purple bricks as she walked up the nearly deserted main street. Several Model T's and one Model A Ford were parked on the sides of the road. It was unlikely they had been driven for days. A monster hurricane had blown away Flagler's Overseas Railroad. Though Key West had been spared, Key Largo had not. Rumor had it there were bodies hanging from the trees there and in Homestead.

The storm of 1935 changed everything.

As Eva walked left on Fleming Street, she could hear the voices of fishermen drinking in one of the hole-in-the-wall bars. They always talked loud, at least that's the way it seemed because the night was quiet except for a rooster's occasional crow and the rustling of trees.

The red brick pharmacy on the corner of Simonton, with its polished oak counters, was dark. There were lights on upstairs and a thin, lacy curtain waved lazily outside an open window. She knew she shouldn't, but she would wait for Ramón in the dark house that belonged to a man who hoped and prayed Eva would soon marry him.

There were no street lamps, but the moon was bright enough that Eva could be recognized by anyone who knew her. There aren't any secrets in a small town – not for long anyhow. She knew the whispers had already begun and that she was in the middle of doing what her *mother had incessantly warned her not to do – make a mess of her life. Crossing over to Southard and then Ashe Street, without hesitation she turned down Olivia because the shadows there would more likely hide her than the ones on Rocky Road. Bayview Park was just bright enough from the moonlight that she continued on underneath the trees just in case someone was sitting on their balcony. Swiftly, quietly, she walked on the balls of her feet so as not to make any noise as she crossed Virginia Street. The latch on the gate clicked when she pushed down on the steel clasp with her thumb. The hinges squeaked as she slipped through and closed it as quietly as she could.*

Above the mailbox to the left of the door were, in brass, the numbers 2929. Without turning on any lights, she climbed the stairs, washed her face with water from a pitcher beside a porcelain basin in the hallway and went out to the balcony where it was cooler. Slightly out of breath from her walk and the climb up the stairs, she lay down on the wicker sofa and looked out at the Big Dipper that always pointed toward the North Star as it spun its way around the sky. She knew that she and Ramón would have to leave town and go north before too long. How, she didn't know without the train, or what they would do after they left.

Ramón, trying to walk nonchalantly, crossed the park and jumped over the short fence. The door wasn't locked – not many were in 1936 in Key West.

It took Lisa, Matt and Frank a while to make the place comfortable, but with a lot of fresh paint, new tile in the kitchen, a completely re-built bathroom, they had been able to put most of their furniture where it belonged.

All said and done things were going well. Granted, using a rented jackhammer to take out the cement slab in the backyard, was not going to be any picnic. The roots of a Poinciana tree had cracked the concrete so badly that it needed to be replaced in order to put an outdoor grill, table and chairs underneath.

At the Blue Heaven Outdoor Theatre, Lisa was starring in a musical comedy, *Clouds Over the Sunshine Inn*, that was doing well. Hair dyed blonde, she was playing the part of sexpot, Laura, who seduces the fiancé of the hotel owner's daughter.

That's all Lisa would tell her two roommates because she didn't want to spoil the show for them. Of course, they had a pretty good idea what the plot was after hearing her recite lines. Matt would accompany her on the guitar so she could rehearse her songs.

Before Ramón's arrival, Eva had, once again, been weighing her options and thinking about her predicament. It was obvious how much Andrew loved her and how beneficial a marriage would be to someone of his wealth at a time when there wasn't any money and the world was in a financial depression. Things were going to be especially difficult in Key West now that there was no Overseas Railroad. But the one she should marry and the one who made her sneak around were not the same. Her young body was already heated at the thought of his shadow easily bouncing over the front gate.

Using the jackhammer was exhausting work. Lisa had tried to help the boys, but it shook her more than it broke apart the cement. Despite how much fun it was to watch her try, as much as it pissed her off, she had resigned herself to the fact that she could only help by putting on her work gloves and lifting the broken pieces into a wheelbarrow and carting them to the commercial dumpster. For Matt and Frank, as wicked as the work was, looking at a comely, sweaty female, occasionally catching a glimpse of her from the side through a blouse that was unbuttoned one too many, kept it about as sexy as hard labor can be.

Coming up the stairs two at a time, Ramón's crooked smile and sparkling eyes filled Eva with an exuberance that could only be satisfied by that primal act they were about to engage in. Slowly he undid her dress and let it fall to the floor leaving only a slip to cover her. Lifting it over her head, she stood naked in the faint moonlight that filtered in. His eyes, well adjusted to the darkness, saw all of her before she kissed him with a tenderness that surprised him as eager as they were.

Not expected back until the following day, Andrew knew something was not quite right. He could sense it when he found the front door slightly ajar. Something didn't smell right, either. From upstairs came the muffled sound of lovemaking and the unmistakable sound of Eva.

Ramón was on top of her when Eva whispered, "Ramón, did you hear that, that click? Ramón!"

During those last few seconds, he was incapable of stopping the final thrusts of the climax that was rising from within him as Andrew crept up the steps. At the same time, Eva froze, eyes wide, sensing danger.

They say you don't hear the gunshot that kills you, but they both felt the surreal blast from a 38-Special that penetrated their chests simultaneously. Not only had she heard it, Eva had time to see the face of the man who had blown apart their hearts for the brief moment it took their brains to die along with the rest of them. It was the face of a person so twisted by the discovery of betrayal that he looked like the devil himself. She wished she could say something before everything went black in the pooling red blood.

Lisa's arms felt like they were about to fall off when she pulled a particularly large chunk of concrete up from the ground. "Oh my God! Oh my fucking God!" was all she could mouth to herself as she stared at the grinning skeleton without a nose looking up at her through sockets where eyeballs had once been.

Covering her mouth with her hands, she backed up in small steps not knowing what to think. Momentarily paralyzed, she began yelling over the sound of the jackhammer at Matt who was taking a break while Frank busted up more concrete.

Flying high above snow-covered fields with only the peaks of the jagged Rocky Mountains visible in the far distance, Frank and Lisa were cruising at 270 knots at an altitude of 20,500 feet on their way from Miami to Aspen, Colorado, in 1386 Zulu, their recently purchased turboprop Beech King Air CargoLiner. Sitting in the right chair of the pressurized cabin, she was typing on her laptop while he, in the left seat fidgeted with the trim and made a slight course correction before asking how the new manuscript was coming along. This would be Lisa's second historical mystery novel set in Key West and her publisher, Shirrel Rhoades, was anxious to read her latest. The title was: *THE WALLS HAD EARS, Murder at 2929.*

"This book writing isn't easy. I'm at the part where we call the police and I haven't decided how our encounter with the murderer should go."

In addition to live theatre, Lisa had discovered that she enjoyed letting her imagination go, making stories up, thinking up scenarios, mixing fact and fiction. Though Frank, Matt and she actually had bought the house at 2929 Virginia Street, which they did fix up, the part about finding the skeletons was completely fictional. Of course, in the novel she would change a lot of the details, including names, yet there would remain certain elements of truth in the setting and characters.

During the years the three of them had lived in the old conch house they had renovated, Frank had slowly grown on her. She and Matt often stayed up late, sharing a joint after work at the bar, and they always had fun conversations, but he didn't scratch the itch that Frank mysteriously caused. "Love," go figure. When Matt, out of the blue, was offered a recording contract, meaning touring, he sold them his share. With jubilation shaded by a twinge of sadness, he wished them the best before packing up and heading to Nashville. They'd stay in touch.

In New York City, of all places, after a drop-off at La Guardia in the old Beech, Frank and Lisa had gone to see Sutton Foster in the revival of *Anything Goes*. During the big number, it just seemed natural for him to rest his hand on her thigh, and, riding on the downtown "C" train, they both instinctively knew where this was going on their way back to the Inn On Twenty-Third Street in the Chelsea area. One thing had led to another, and together they leveraged all they had to buy the relatively new plane, which was really a cool piece of equipment.

"Okay." Lisa said, "The police come to see the two skeletons, one on top of the other, and exhume them, the news making the front page of *The Key West Citizen* ... or maybe the trio doesn't call the police?"

"Maybe they leave the bones alone and try to find out themselves what had happened? No, they'd have to call the cops, but I doubt the police would do much investigating. There are details I need to figure out.

"I think I'll have a drug dealer living in the Bahamas as one suspect who almost kills our heroes – before they confront a demented doctor who moved from 2929 Virginia to Savannah.

"What do you think?" Lisa said before leaning over and kissing Frank, putting her hand in between his legs, feeling his response.

"Lisa, I think this is wrong, wrong, wrong. How many times already have we joined the mile high club?"

"Once more," she said as he watched her wiggle out of her jeans and unbutton her flannel shirt so he could put his arms around her bare flesh. On autopilot, she undid his pants and slipped on top of him.

An hour later, more or less, filled with a cargo of fresh seafood, they cleared Independence Pass and, with full flaps, put the nose and the landing gear down for the steep approach to the lone runway that had recently been cleared by a snowplow. After touchdown, men from the local fish market wearing ski parkas and lamb's wool lined boots, began unloading the Styrofoam containers from the cargo door.

6.
Better Times Than These

William R. Burkett, Jr.

All the uproar in this new century about police misbehavior is sadly ironic in view of an ugly little case I got involved with in the early '90s on vacation in Key West. Different times than these, but a shadow of coming events.

Julie and I were sleeping late in the "master stateroom" of Buchinsky's big houseboat, worn out after a day of full-bore touristing. Hemingway's House, Tennessee Williams' House, the Audubon House Museum, Old Town, historic cigar-making places, a dozen T-shirt shops featuring Conch Republic memorabilia; she even dragged me around looking for places Jose Marti stayed while planning his Cuban revolution. My pale Northwest hide was doubly burned from that foray and a day on the bonefish flats in Buchinksy's blazing-fast flats boat.

My old boss with the Pennsylvania State Police, and present silent partner in my Seattle detective agency, was channeling his inner Travis McGee and finally persuaded me to visit. This wasn't Fort Lauderdale, his boat wasn't custom and was seven feet shorter than McGee's. But he figured *Double Dipper* was close enough for a twice-retired State Police colonel.

Where he found Navy-strength Plymouth Gin –

meaning the proof required by the Royal Navy – I have no idea. I don't remember McGee specifying Royal Navy Proof. But it made excellent good gin-tonics that eased the pain of sunburn and exhaustion from keeping up with Julie. She had urged sunscreen on me and had no mercy on my sunburned hide in the big master suite bed. Being on vacation roused her libido. It was one of those pain-pleasure deals that made me wonder if she was a closet dominatrix.

When voices in the main cabin woke me, she looked angelic asleep. Me, I felt like ten miles of rough road. I eased out of bed, hit the head, pulled on sweat pants and a brand-new Conch Republic T-shirt and followed my nose to the aroma of fresh coffee in the galley.

Buchinksy, in shorts and bare-chested, with a silver thatch of chest hair decorating his bronzed torso, was in the main cabin with a visitor: a coal-black man dressed for church in a cheap but immaculate blue suit. Despite the icy air from Buchinksy's big AC, he looked sweaty and uncomfortable.

"Come on in, Eddie," the colonel said. "This is Pete, one of the best Flats fishing guides there is. Even you could catch a bonefish or snook with Pete on the job."

The visitor and I shook hands. He was scrawny and looked underfed, but his hands were big as mine, armored in callus. But his grip was gentle.

"Mr. Hummel, sir."

"Call me Eddie. Don't let Buchinsky talk you into taking me out. I'd ruin your reputation. I've lived in the Northwest for twenty five years and still haven't caught my first steelhead."

He smiled at that, but the smile was strained. It wasn't just the suit making him uncomfortable; I had interrupted serious talk. I was about to suggest I go forward and give them privacy but Buchinksy beat me to the punch.

"Sit down, Eddie, I want you to hear this. Pete, Eddie's still a practicing detective. And my partner. Run it down for him."

Pete heaved a ragged sigh and started in. A teenage boy from Bahama Village – a Key West neighborhood, not the islands east of here – had headed for Miami with a couple of friends for a lark. It was a long haul – Miami is farther away than Cuba, where teenagers used to go on the ferry before Castro – but his folks thought nothing of it. They were all good kids, excellent students, well-mannered, not into drugs, close to high school graduation and wanting to stretch their wings. A teenage rite of passage. Thoughts of trouble never crossed the parents' minds.

Next time they heard his voice, very upset and anxious, he was calling from a Homestead Jail phone. They weren't clear why he had been arrested. With a suspicion never far from the minds of black Americans, they thought it had been his skin color.

"Homestead?" I said. "Not Miami? Where's Homestead?"

"It's a small town near Miami," Buchinsky said. "Being an old trooper, I was guessing traffic stop. But the other kids weren't with him. They were back home by the time he called from the jail."

"What did they say?"

"They stopped for barbecue and a local girl picked him up," Pete said. "They didn't want to leave him but ..."

"But his tongue was hanging out," Buchinsky said. "I was young myself, Pete. So were you."

"I didn't talk to the others till my friend came back from Homestead," Pete said to me. "They jumped in their car and went straight up there when their son called."

"Okay," I said. "What did they find out?"

And here's where the story got strange. When they got

to the jail, officials said they had never heard of him. He wasn't there. He had never been there. No records in the computer; can't help you.

Pete paused. Then, "My friend almost had to drag his wife out of the jail – she was building up a head of steam that her son called from there and they were calling him a liar."

"Jailors wouldn't like that," Buchinksy said. "They were all white, I suppose." Pete nodded. "No-win situation. Good thing he got her out of there."

"What happened next?"

"They hung around that barbecue place asking kids if they knew their boy or had seen him. Thing is, most of the kids there were white, which made them nervous. Finally they just came home."

"Did they ask to see the arrest docket?"

Pete frowned. "What's that? All they said was he wasn't in the computer."

"Police keep arrest dockets that are public records," I said. "The idea is this is a democracy and police can't just 'vanish' people like a police state."

Pete looked hopeful for a moment, until Buchinksy cleared his throat. "Eddie, when's the last time you looked at a docket?"

"Years. I've got the contacts now if I need arrest information."

"About what I thought. Welcome to the computer age. Much more efficient."

"I hate computers," I said. "You telling me they replaced docket sheets with damned computers?"

"Well a lot of jurisdictions have. Dade County is a witch's brew. The sheriff runs the police in Miami and all unincorporated areas. Homestead's got its own jail but I bet they link right up to Metro Dade."

"You're the retired state cop," I said. "Don't you have

any Florida Highway Patrol contacts from all your junkets?"

"I do, in fact. And that's not a bad idea." Pete had been following this with a blank look. "More Cokes in the fridge," Buchinsky told him. "Help yourself while I make some calls." He had a phone by the sofa, and rummaged in an end table for an address book. Pete got another Coke. I refilled my coffee. It was a pleasure watching Buchinsky work again. Smooth small talk prefacing a staccato of direct questions. It wasn't a pleasure to watch his face grow stonier with each answer.

"A major in Tallahassee I attended an FBI seminar with," he said. "In charge of their computer networks. He verified no entry with the boy's name in Homestead or Miami-Dade. And no, there is no paper docket in Homestead."

"What does it all mean?" Pete asked quietly.

Buchinsky was no bull-shitter. "It doesn't look good," he said. To me, "Before you started playing cops and robbers I recruited you off a newspaper. You got any contacts with the Miami *Herald*?"

"I may." I moved over to the phone and called Maury Teller at the Seattle *P-I* city desk, a number I memorized long ago. It was early on the West Coast and he was cranky, but he came through as he usually did. A former co-worker of ours among the ink-stained wretches had migrated to the sun and risen to bureau chief in one of the *Herald's* bureaus.

"What am I asking him?"

He leaned over and put his hand on Pete's knee. "There's no confirmation yet, Pete. So let's hope this is a bum steer." To me, "Toll-keepers on Card Sound Bridge fished the body of a young black male out of the water. A trooper responded. The body was transported to the Monroe County medical examiner's office in Marathon.

My guy is going to check into it for me, but he says the *Herald* runs an efficient cop-shop and should have information by now."

"Running the daily trap-line," I said. It took me a couple calls to connect with Joe Crankshaw. He said he'd heard I went over to the enemy and worked for cops now. I told him that was very old news and I was in business for myself now but I wondered how the *Herald* hired a hack like him. With the pleasantries out of the way he wanted to know what I wanted.

"You never make social calls, so get on with it," is how he put it. So I laid it out for him. He put me on hold to check with cop-shop reporters. Sure enough, they had the bare details already.

"The ME in that two-palm-tree town is already calling it suicide," he said. "Cause of death strangulation. They won't waste much time on this. Sound like the kid who vanished from the jail?"

"I don't know, but the timing is awful close." I replayed his words. "Strangulation, not drowning? Any water in his lungs?"

Joe laughed. "Same old nasty suspicious mind, Eddie. They might not even bother with that detail."

If they were certified medical examiners, my bet was they would. I worked a famous hoodlum "suicide" in Commencement Bay where his lungs proved full of *fresh* water when the feds didn't buy the first take. Those kinds of embarrassments get around professional communities. Professionals would cover their bets.

I didn't learn I was right about that until I was home in Seattle, when Buchinsky called foaming at the mouth to tell me that the case was closed with an "indeterminate" ruling as manner of death.

But we knew within the hour that day that it was probably the missing boy. Buchinksy's Tallahassee contact called back to fill in details held back from the media. The boy's billfold with his driver's license in it, and a thick paperback novel, had been found on the bridge a couple miles out when the trooper searched for where the boy went in. The Monroe County ME would be calling his parents to establish a positive ID.

Pete's coal-black face developed an ashen cast when he got the news. Buchinsky silently put a big arm around his shoulders, bucking him up, before he slipped on deck shoes and a shirt and went with him to alert the parents that heartbreak was coming.

They hadn't been gone long when Julie came out looking for coffee, all showered and fresh in her own Conch T and shorts. No shoes, no bra, and that glow of a well-bedded woman. I was scribbling notes on a piece of paper and hated to douse that look, but told her what I was doing – writing lines of investigation – when she asked. She went from glow to intense concentration, and had to hear the whole story.

"My god, Eddie, that's horrible." She gazed off across the marina but she wasn't seeing it. I knew she was thinking of her son back in Seattle. "Are you going to take the case?"

"I can't. I'm not licensed in Florida and I've been away a long time. No contacts. Snoop too hard and *I* might wind up under a bridge."

"What about Buchinsky?"

"That's why I'm writing notes: get the jail phone records to match up any call to the parents. Interview the bridge toll-takers. If somebody took him on the bridge, they might remember a car. Re-interview kids at the barbecue place. Check for water in his lungs."

"Why that? The report says strangled."

"There's different ways to strangle. An improperly applied choke hold for instance. In a prison lockup."

She wasn't as shocked as most would be; she'd spent too many years on hospital staff and read newspaper accounts of that sort of death.

"If there's no paper trail it wouldn't take many key strokes to take him out of their computers," she pinpointed. Medical records were her specialty. "A smart operator would overwrite too, in case of a forensic check."

"I hate computers," I said.

"Well the digital age has dawned, sweetheart."

"Making it harder to catch crooks," I said. "I remember cases where docket entries were the only evidence cops lied about things."

"This stinks!" she said. "Can Buchinsky do anything?"

As it eventually turned out, not much, as he told me when he called about the ME notation there was no water in the boy's lungs. The parents buried their son and mourned in private, and never hired an attorney to file suit and initiate discovery of phone records and such. The Highway Patrol, unlike the State Police, could not dig into local agencies without being asked. His buddy in Tallahassee said there was no interest in creating a sensation in South Florida. No arrest docket, no computer entry, no prisoner in Homestead. That poor kid found under the bridge down the road, dead of strangulation? Nope, never heard of him.

That was my introduction to the digital age as adapted by police agencies. Buchinsky said he was glad he was retired. I said I wished I was. Who knows what goes on now out of public view? Call me Luddite if you want, but I think pen-and-ink police blotters represented better times than these.

7.
THE IMPRESARIO

Hal Howland

*F*uck.

Monroe County homicide detective Rich Castillo put down the phone and stared out at the coconut palm swaying too close to his office window. He had just received word that his partner, Sergeant Alvin Varela, had been shot in the right leg the previous night in a Stock Island convenience store.

Varela was off duty at the time and accidentally interrupted an attempted holdup. He managed to kick the gun out of a desperate robber's hand and, with the proprietor's help, restrained the teenage crackhead until backup arrived. The minor hero was now lying in a bed at Lower Keys Medical Center and was expected to be off the street – and off the salsa dance floor at El Meson de Pepe – for eight weeks.

As Castillo prepared to walk the short distance to the hospital to visit his friend, he lamented two sudden realities and could not decide which was worse: (1) the detective would temporarily be saddled with a new, probably younger and less compatible partner, and (2) the Rich Castillo Band, in which Alvin Varela played percolating bass alongside Castillo's irresistible drumming, would have to cancel two months' gigs. Unlike most Key West bands, Castillo's outfit played mostly original music and, since that music featured exquisite four-part harmonies and thoughtful arrangements, actually rehearsed. Castillo would not even consider hiring someone to sub for one half of the Keys' premier rhythm section. The loss of moonlighting income was hardly a disaster for Castillo, given that local club owners knew they could get away with paying their nonunion entertainers nineteen sixties wages; but the absence of Varela's companionship and of all four band members' main creative outlet was a bummer. Castillo dreaded delivering the news to guitarists Ed Carlyle and Vladimir "Velvet" Voznesensky, but it was too early in the day to call them – unlike Castillo and Varela, the two freelancers had no day job to fill in the musical gaps – and the drummer wanted to be able to tell them more about Varela's condition.

Having confirmed that his partner was not permanently injured and was in typically good spirits, Castillo returned to his office to call the other two and to consider his immediate future.

Rich Castillo kept up his chops with regular workouts on a set of rubberized wood practice pads that his neighbors on narrow Poorhouse Lane could not hear, but earnest repetition in a ticking studio was no substitute for the quick reflexes needed in the charged atmosphere of the gig. After a history of declining offers from Key West's assortment of lackluster musicians, the University of Miami alum decided to throw caution to the wind. It did not take long for word to get out that the respected drummer was temporarily available and for his cell phone to begin ringing at rude hours.

As he had expected, Lieutenant Rich Castillo was handed an interim partner straight out of the academy. The county sheriff and his wife, friends of the kid's widowed mom, prevailed on Castillo to take him on as a personal favor. When after a few rides together Castillo reported that the kid had uttered the most offensive racist and xenophobic language he had ever heard, the sheriff reassigned the rookie to guard detail at the little county airport: the departmental purgatory for problem children. The remainder of Alvin Varela's convalescence was filled with another new recruit whose only drawback was her stunning Mediterranean beauty. Castillo even noticed a disturbing resemblance to his girlfriend, massage therapist Victoria Landini – an observation Castillo wisely kept to himself.

    The first of Castillo's sometime freelance music clients to buttonhole him was the mountainous and entertaining bluesman Elliott "Grizzly" Clatterbuck, who following years of shuttling between Key West and his native Atlanta had secured himself a house gig at a renovated former jazz club at the corner of Front and Whitehead Streets. El Fumadero Cubano occupied the floor above the owner's cigar shop and offered a menu of stale air, bland food, and live blues six nights a week. Clatterbuck's regular drummer was a loudmouthed drunk who kept his gig solely by providing the P.A. system that broadcast the club's uninvited repertoire to the cruise-ship passengers disembarking across the street at Mallory Square, and Griz was eager to capitalize on any opportunity to offer his listeners a bit of variety in addition to steady timekeeping.

    Castillo had enjoyed playing with Clatterbuck sporadically over the years and slipped back into the bassist's old-school driver's seat as if he had never left. It was actually a relief just to sit back and groove without thinking about intricate vocal parts and the many other details of leading his own band. Castillo hated playing the student-quality house drum set, soiled as it was by dust, cigar ashes, sticky cocktail stains, and drumstick shavings, but its presence made the amateurish situation that much easier to walk away from when the night was over.

Less tolerable was the behavior of the omnipresent club owner, Nicky Molinari. The tall, pale, muscular man of no discernible hair color paced through the room a hundred times a night between trips downstairs to check on the cigar store. Molinari sported a uniform of sorts, consisting of brown alligator cowboy boots, tight blue jeans, any of several tight dark Harley-Davidson T-shirts, and any of several nonmatching paisley bandannas worn as headscarves. Patrons often mistook the proprietor for a busboy or for one of their own, and Molinari did not seem bothered by their reaction to his ludicrous appearance. When Molinari addressed the musicians it generally was with a stream of snarling negativity regarding their volume – always too loud or too soft, despite unchanged settings – or their curious habit of expecting to be treated as human beings when approaching the bar during a break. Molinari thought nothing of ascending the stage in the middle of a song and taking over the mixing board to ensure that defenseless pedestrians on the sidewalks below were gaining the full benefit of his musical ignorance. Equally amusing was Molinari's penchant for calling individual musicians *brother,* as if they had something in common besides the perilous economy.

Financially, Nicky Molinari was the worst offender among Key West's notoriously cheap club owners. To afford six weekly nights of live music featuring not just typical guitar trios but full five- and six-piece bands with keyboards and horns, Molinari paid rock-bottom money to the dregs of the local scene. Grizzly Clatterbuck, who suffered various health problems and who a few years before had been effectively homeless, had rushed to accept his steady weekend gig despite the insulting pay; he was considered the club's headliner. The other three nights brought in musicians who would have been hard pressed to find professional employment of any kind in a real city. They did not complain about the bread because they knew even less about the business than they did about their craft.

On a break one evening after enduring the lesbian bartender's routinely surly reception, Castillo walked outside to breathe some fresh air. He went down the steps to the street, where he encountered Molinari milling about in front of his deserted shop. The club owner kept in constant cell-phone contact with his upstairs staff, who shared his opinion that the musicians who kept his business open were at best unwelcome visitors. Sensing Castillo's discomfort, Molinari sidled over to him and asked if everything was all right.

Years of bandleading had taught Rich Castillo to interact with club owners only when absolutely necessary. But his itinerant relationship with Molinari, who struck him as just the latest in a long line of arrogant fools hoping to make a killing exploiting Key West's clueless tourists, inspired the drummer to make an exception. He did not expect the conversation to go well, and it did not.

"You might want to offer your bartender a brief lesson in etiquette," Castillo smiled.

"Oh?" Molinari replied. "How's that, brother?"

Castillo described the treatment he had just received, which both men knew was typical.

"Well, my customers come first," Molinari said defensively.

"Yes," Castillo answered, estimating that he had been performing in nightclubs when his inquisitor was still sucking his thumb, "but the room is practically empty, and, as usual, Corrine went out of her way to avoid me as if she actually had something to do."

"Maybe she did."

"She was standing around talking with a girlfriend and

ignoring customers besides myself."

"You're not my customer. You're my employee."

"Nonsense," Castillo replied. "I am an independent contractor, like the guy who delivered this now lukewarm Heineken. You pay us in cash, off the books, from what I hear, and you don't contribute to our health care or pension. That's not an employer-employee relationship."

Molinari stepped back and smiled. "You know, brother, I'm pretty generous with you guys."

Castillo suppressed a laugh.

"You get a free meal and two free drinks a night. That could stop."

"We wish it would," Castillo countered. "In exchange for your lousy food, your slow service, and the same beer we have at home, we'd prefer a living wage."

Molinari, who knew nothing of Castillo's day job, drew himself fully upright. "Have you ever owned a restaurant?" he asked.

"Of course not," Castillo replied. "Have you?"

"Look, pal, I don't think I like your tone."

Castillo chuckled. "Well, if your drummer knew anything about tuning, maybe his crappy instruments would resonate more to your liking."

Failing to get the joke, Molinari edged forward.

The Miami native stood his ground. "Do you have any idea what musicians earn in the real world? You cannot continue treating us as second-class citizens."

A long silence ensued.

Finally Molinari said, "Well, that's your perception. Everyone else who plays here seems perfectly happy to do so."

"Actually," Castillo replied, "that's not quite the case. First of all, I'm here tonight only as a favor to an old acquaintance. Second, I wouldn't hire any of those hacks upstairs to play a backyard barbeque. And third, I know for a fact that every musician who's ever played here thinks you're a complete asshole. Next question?"

Molinari seemed on the verge of employing his impressive musculature. "You know, I don't think this is working out."

Castillo laughed. "Oh, you noticed that? Well, at least we agree on something, albeit for different reasons. But as I said, you can't fire someone who doesn't work for you."

"OK, pal," Molinari exhaled inches from Castillo's face, "when this next set is over you can take your drums and get the fuck out of here."

Smiling politely, Castillo answered, "Well, once again, I wouldn't own that drum set if you were giving it away. But you may be certain that I have no further need for your company." Castillo poured his unfinished beer into the gutter, tossed the bottle into a recycling bin, and walked back upstairs.

At the end of the night, the band as usual had to wait nearly an hour to get paid. Castillo pocketed his chump change, grabbed his stick bag, and headed for the door.

Molinari was awaiting Castillo on the landing. "We need to talk," he said with authority.

"No, we don't," Castillo smiled as he headed down the steps.

"Don't walk away from me, pal," Molinari said.

Castillo stopped, turned, and considered his options. A simple display of his badge probably would silence Molinari for good: it was widely known that the businessman owed money to vendors all over town, including the sign painter who had eradicated all wistful traces of the defunct jazz club. And of course Castillo never went anywhere without a firearm. His fatigue, from the gig and from Molinari's tedious existence, was another factor. But the idiot was offering a fun epilogue to an otherwise worthless evening. "Look, man, I didn't ask to be here, and

I definitely won't be back. But let me give you a piece of advice."

Molinari gripped the banister.

Castillo continued: "A year from now, when you're sitting in bankruptcy court, dressed, I would recommend, not as Willie Nelson's bus driver but rather as someone who might expect to be taken seriously, maybe you'll consider finding yourself an honorable way to make a living. Playing impresario, that is, ripping off educated musicians doesn't seem to be your calling."

Molinari made a move toward Castillo.

"And unless you'd like to add a few criminal charges into the mix," the cop continued while reaching under his shirttail, "I suggest you keep your hands to yourself."

Molinari stood trembling with clenched fists. "Fuck you!" he screamed.

Castillo laughed. "Exactly." He turned, descended the stairs, crossed the street, and got in his minivan. He lowered the windows and sat a while in the sea breeze, letting the embarrassing night sink in. The musician had never allowed one of these clowns to bait him, and he swore to himself that it would not happen again. He started the engine and drove home.

Nine months later El Fumadero Cubano went out of business, but the touristy smoke shop remained open. Nicky Molinari contented himself with the commerce of day-trippers whose fantasies convinced them that buying a thirty-dollar cigar a hundred yards from their waiting cruise ship, having seen nothing of the real Key West, would somehow imbue them with the mystique left lingering in the jasmine air by the town's long-dead literary heroes. When news of Molinari's fiscal dealings became public – it turned out that, like many of his colleagues, the club owner had supported his own fantasy with a thriving sideline in pharmaceutical sales – no one bothered to say *I told you so.*

Nicky Molinari turned up dead from blunt trauma late one night in the alley behind the Red Garter strip club. Rich Castillo and Alvin Varela got the call. As they awaited the forensic team to make sense of Molinari's multiple injuries, the two cops agreed that the perpetrator could have been anyone from the sign painter to the guy who used to deliver the Heineken. They ruled out most of their fellow musicians, simply because people in that profession tend to be unfit pacifists. By dawn the murder weapon was determined to have been a heavy, probably wooden object such as a baseball bat.

The next time Rich Castillo heard from Elliott "Grizzly" Clatterbuck, it was via a Facebook posting announcing the bluesman's new residency at a popular nightspot in Tokyo. Neither Castillo nor Varela, who was equally particular about the quality of his instruments, would have had any reason to know that Clatterbuck's bastardized Fender bass guitar had recently been thoroughly cleaned up and was now available for purchase on eBay.

8.
FOUR FINGERS AND THE ACERBIC FILM CRITIC

Shirrel Rhoades

A crowd had gathered at the Porch, a casual bar on the first floor of a tree-shaded mansion at the corner of Caroline and Duval. This popular watering hole was ground zero for the annual Key West Film Festival. But this afternoon a barrier of gesticulating cops and yellow crime scene tape helped keep the rubberneckers at bay.

Word had it a movie star was dead. When pressed for details by a *Citizen* reporter, a police department insider whispered that a Hollywood A-lister – Race Collins, star of that new remake of *Key Largo* – had been murdered by person or persons unknown.

"Poisoned," he added.

"A remake of *Key Largo*," muttered Police Chief Johnny Leigh. "That's sacrilege. I might've killed him myself given the opportunity." Cop humor.

Only five people had the opportunity by the Chief's

reckoning – the bartender, the waitress, and Race Collins's three drinking companions: the movie's producer, Race's sexy co-star, and an acerbic film critic from MovieMadness.com.

The death of a famous movie star was too dicey a proposition to get wrong. As a tourist destination, Key West ranks number five among Yahoo!'s travel info searches. Johnny Leigh's job could be at stake if he botched this one.

So he called Wharton "Four Fingers" Dalessandro.

Although not official, Four Fingers – a nickname that came from a missing digit on his left hand – was a good detective because he was lazy. That is, he didn't like to work very hard. Maybe that's the same thing.

Years ago, when he was an NYPD cop, he'd built a reputation for quickly solving crimes. Homicides in particular. As he put it, murder cases might be complicated but their solutions were often simple when you looked at it the right way. So to avoid a lot of footwork and filling out forms his deductive reasoning seemed to kick into high gear, usually figuring out whodunit in four minutes or less. An *NY Post* reporter had actually timed him.

"It's just a matter of looking at the clues," he'd been quoted in the *Post*'s story.

He'd been a bit embarrassed by the headline.

A Study in Blue:
Sherlock Holmes
On the Lower East Side

Not that this publicity mattered much. He'd got shot, pensioned out on full disability, and retired to Key West.

Here on this spit of limestone 150 miles south of Miami, but only 90 miles north of Havana, he played chess with his chum Dunk Reid, painted houses in his spare time, and occasionally helped Police Chief Johnny Leigh solve a crime. Not that there were many homicides in this Southernmost town in the continental US, despite what you read in all those mystery books by Michael Haskins and Bill Craig.

A local shrink (who had once been in charge of Belleview) described Dalessandro as a kind of *idiot savant*, having weird wiring in his brain that allowed him to figure out murders by using mental shortcuts. "A functional Rain Man," he called him.

Race Collins had been the featured guest of this year's film festival.

According to studio publicity, the actor had been discovered by a big-name Hollywood producer while parking cars at a fancy restaurant on Sunset Strip. Truth was, Race Collins (né Ralph Cottersly) had been arrested while stealing a Lamborghini that belonged to said producer, Lawrence Weinstein of New Caledonia Pictures. When Larry saw the car thief in a police lineup, he was so impressed by the young man's charm and charisma he dropped his complaint and signed the future Race Collins to a five-year contract.

That was two years and four pictures ago. The first movie was a rom-com titled *Mr. Lovable*. The next two were fairly forgettable, *Menace at Midnight* and *Fast Track 5*. Then came his big breakthrough role in a remake of *Key Largo*. Based on the 1948 classic about a man trapped in a hotel with a gangster during a hurricane, it starred Race in the Humphrey Bogart role, alongside Big John Billingsley and newcomer Vera Storm.

Key Largo was getting a sneak preview at the film festival. Race Collins was man of the hour, having signed a new management contract with ICM. His price was now $10 mil a picture. *Variety* reported he was up for the lead in a new *Star Wars* movie. Rumor had it he and Vera Storm were sharing a room.

Now Race was dead.

He looked nothing like Humphrey Bogart, thought Four Fingers Dalessandro as he eyed the corpse. The body was still sprawled on the floor where it had toppled from a barstool after downing a drink prophetically named Death In the Afternoon. A mixture of absinthe and champagne, it was invented in 1935 by Ernest Hemingway. An appropriate drink for this island where the great writer once lived. The recipe included the instruction to "drink three to five of these slowly."

Race barely finished one before keeling over dead.

"May as well let me meet your suspects," said Four Fingers.

"Persons of interest," corrected the Police Chief Johnny Leigh.

"Whatever."

First one paraded out was the bartender who had mixed the drinks. With his shoulder-length blond hair and golden tan, Ronald Strumbo looked more like a thirtysomething surfer dude than a mixologist who worked long hours in a dusky saloon. His face displayed a sharp, thin nose and droopy eyes. His tats were the hand-inked kind you get in prison.

Needless to say, he proclaimed his innocence. "I poured a jigger of absinthe into a flute of iced Moet," he said. "Just like the drink recipe calls for."

"A popular drink?" asked Four Fingers.

"Never had a call for one before. Had to look it up in the recipe book we keep behind the bar. Only had one bottle of absinthe on the shelf, just enough in it for the four drinks they ordered. They'd been shit outta luck if they wanted another round."

"I thought absinthe was illegal," mused Four Finger, not much of a drinker.

"The old wormwood stuff was outlawed for over seventy-five years, but the ban was lifted in the '90s."

Four Finger frowned. "That's what they were drinking, just absinthe and champagne?"

"That's right. Not a drop of rat poison in the recipe," the bartender smirked.

"A comedian," commented Chief Johnny Leigh. It wasn't a compliment.

Next came the waitress, a twenty-two-year-old college dropout with a scary Goth look: dark eye shadow and black lipstick contrasted against vampirish white makeup. Mary Rackovich's ears and nose had more piercings than the dartboard on the far wall. "The drinks were on my tray for maybe ten seconds as I stepped from the bar to that actor's table," she whined. "No reason for me to poison him. I was hoping for a big tip."

Lawrence "Larry" Weinstein was a portly man in his late sixties, evidenced by the wispy white hair surrounding a bowling-ball-shaped head. A well-known Hollywood producer, he was the name behind *Horror House II* and *Gremlins in the Garden*. But the *Key Largo* remake was said to be his crowning achievement, promising a big opening weekend.

"What can you tell us?" said Johnny Leigh.

Weinstein scowled at the Police Chief and his digitally impaired friend. "Don't look at me," he huffed. "I had millions tied up in that kid. The studio had already green-lighted a sequel to *Key Largo*. I was gonna call it *For Whom the Boat Trolls*. A seafaring adventure."

Johnny Leigh rolled his eyes disapprovingly. Obviously a Hemingway fan. "And you?" he said to the pretty woman seated between the producer and the film critic.

The blonde introduced herself as Sarah Kapinsky – but Weinstein quickly corrected her: "Vera Storm," he said. Then to the others, "Vera is co-star of *Key Largo*. Don't you think she looks like a young Lauren Bacall?"

"Maybe those sloe eyes," the Chief allowed. Being polite.

"Race and I were engaged," she said.

"You were banging him," the producer snapped. "He hadn't popped the question."

"He would've if somebody hadn't killed him," Sarah/Vera groused. She didn't sound all that broken up about her would-be fiancé's demise.

Four Fingers turned to the film critic. "What do you make of this?"

Antoine Silbey needed no introduction. He reviews appeared regularly online, his byline familiar to moviegoers. "I'm just an innocent bystander," he said. "I was here to interview him for my column."

"On MovieMania.com?"

"That's right. Are you a reader?"

"Now and then."

"How nice."

Johnny Leigh interjected. "Any idea who might have had a reason to kill Race Collins?"

"Just about anyone who has seen his new picture," the film critic replied in a condescending tone. He was a gnome-like man with heavy brows and thick glasses perched atop a razor-thin nose. He had a sleepy look, as if bored with the tragic events surrounding him.

"Does that include you?" Johnny Leigh asked pointedly.

"Most definitely me. But I didn't do it. Didn't bring any cyanide with me today."

Four Fingers picked up the near-empty glass on the table. "Is this the movie star's drink?"

"What's left of it," Weinstein confirmed. "He gulped it down like a thirsty man in a desert. We hadn't even clinked glasses."

"He complained that his throat was parched," said Sarah/Vera. "He'd just given a talk at the San Carlos."

"If you could call that juvenile rambling a talk," shrugged the critic. Not hesitating to speak ill of the dead.

Decidedly unlikable, Four Fingers thought as he delicately swirled the last remnant of liquid in the actor's glass and sniffed at it. "Are you sure he was poisoned?" he asked the Police Chief. "Not a heart attack or a blood clot or a brain embolism?"

"Can't eliminate that. But the 911 call said he'd been poisoned, so we're treating it as a homicide."

"Who made the 911 call?"

"I did," volunteered Antoine Silbey, holding up his iPhone. "Phoned within seconds after he hit the floor."

"You ever interviewed Race Collins before?" asked Four Fingers.

"Yes, once. But it never got published."

"Why not?"

He hesitated. "I was going to reveal his background. But he used his producer here to pressure MovieMadness.com to drop the piece."

"It w-was slander," sputtered Larry Weinstein. "I have a big investment in that boy. No two-bit movie reviewer's gonna jeopardize that!"

"You *had* an investment in Race," pouted Sarah/Vera. "But now it's down the drain just like my engagement."

"You weren't engaged," insisted the producer. "He slept with all his co-stars."

"He said I was special."

"He told them all that. Don't go getting your heart broken over an on-set fling."

"He was going to help me with my career."

Antoine Silby snorted. "Ol' Larry here can do that if you bang him too."

"Really?" A light flickered in her baby blues.

Larry Weinstein offered a raffish smile. "I'm always happy to help a talented young actress like yourself."

"Really?" she repeated. A new plan formulating, it would seem.

Ignoring them, Four Fingers turned back to the film

critic. "What background were you going to reveal?"

"That Ralph Cottersly – Race to you – was a carjacker before Weinstein here discovered him. He'd done time for grand theft auto."

"That's a lie!" shouted the producer.

"Easy to check," commented the Police Chief.

"Well, maybe the boy did have a checkered past," muttered the producer. "But there was no need to dredge it up. He had a bright future ahead of him. Until now." The producer reached for his drink and raised it to his lips, a nervous reaction.

"Don't drink that," warned Four Fingers.

"Why not? I can handle my liquor. That stint in rehab was for pain medication. I have a bad back."

"Have any of you tasted your drinks yet?" said Four Fingers.

"No."

"Huh-uh."

"Not yet. Why?"

"They may be poisoned too."

"Egad!" Larry Weinstein slammed his glass onto the table and snatched his hand away. "Is someone trying to kill us all?"

"Just you and your boy Race, I'd guess."

"You mean I'm safe?" squealed Sarah/Vera.

"Oh, your glass may be poisoned too. But you'd just be collateral damage. Mr. Silbey only had a grudge against the other two."

"Hey, don't look at me. My drink is poisoned too," protested the critic.

"How do you know that, if you haven't tasted it?"

"Well, I assume – "

"And how did you know it was cyanide? That's what you said a moment ago."

"Cyanide?" said Johnny Leigh.

"Race's glass has the faint odor of bitter almonds. A characteristic of cyanide."

Antoine Silbey snarled, "Okay, you got me. But these rich Hollywood bastards had it coming. They got me fired. So I came down here to even the score. Told them I wanted to write a positive review of *Key Largo* to set things right. I'm just sorry I didn't get Weinstein too."

"What about me?" wailed Sarah/Vera.

The critic gave her a disdainful sneer. "Don't worry, honey. You've got a pretty face and big tits. You'll latch onto another career builder soon enough. Doesn't matter that you can't act your way out of a paper bag."

"You're a mean, mean man," she sniffled. "I'm taking acting lessons."

"Stick with ol' Larry here and you won't need them," he said. Vicious to the last.

"Antoine Silby, you're under arrest," stated Police Chief Johnny Leigh, snapping handcuffs onto the film critic's wrists. He read the man his rights, not that it was going to help, given his impromptu confession.

"I can't believe he tried to kill me," sputtered Larry Weinstein, oblivious to the dead star laying at his feet. "Why would he do that?"

"Silbey wanted revenge for you and Race getting him fired. The idea was to poison all four of the drinks to throw suspicion off himself. He, of course, wouldn't taste his Death in the Afternoon, knowing that it was laced with cyanide."

Police Chief Johnny Leigh glanced at his watch. "You're getting slow, Four Fingers. This homicide took you five minutes and forty-five seconds to solve. I timed it."

"May as well keep your stopwatch running. There's more."

"More? You got the killer."

"He had an accomplice. The bartender."

"How do you figure that?"

"Silbey might have been able to slip something into one drink, but not all four. That would have been noticeable. And the waitress didn't have time to do it. That leaves the bartender."

At this point Ronald Strumbo ducked around the wood-scarred bar and ran for the door. But a burly policeman blocked his escape.

"Bet he hasn't been working here long," commented Four Fingers Dalessandro.

"True," Johnny Leigh nodded. "He's extra help hired during the film festival."

"Probably Antoine Silbey's younger brother. They've got the same nose."

"Now that you mention it, I do see a resemblance."

"My nephew," admitted the film critic.

Lawrence Weinstein looked down at the dead movie star on the floor as if seeing him for the first time. "A shame," he sighed. "That boy could've made me millions." Then he glanced up at the man across the table. "Why did you have to murder my star? Couldn't you have just given the movie a bad review?"

"At least this way there won't be a sequel," sneered Antoine Silby, a film critic to the very end.

9. HAND-FED SNAPPING TURTLES

Robert Coburn

The two men docked late that morning in Key West after a quick run down from Miami. A little more than three hours from Coral Gables, blasting along the Intercostal Waterway and cutting through at Seven Mile Bridge. For the Boston Whaler 345 with 900 horses kicking ass, it was just another day in the office. The dockmaster directed the boat to its berth. Pier D over near Turtle Kraals. A rare availability, he'd added.

"Need to refuel?" he asked over the radio.

"No thanks, we topped up in Miami," Ed Beasly said. "Got a 450 mile range so we're good for the return."

"Have a nice day then."

"You, too."

Beasly backed the Whaler into its slip while his friend, Gary Pratt, handled the tie-off lines.

They were business associates. Their wives were close friends. It was a nice sociable arrangement and would've remained so had Gary not been screwing Ed's wife, Joan. Which pretty much accounted for the old song currently stuck in Ed's head. But with a slight lyrical change. *Fifty ways to kill your wife's lover.* He'd sung it to himself all the way to Key West. So far he hadn't come across the right one.

They'd run down for the weekend. Boys' night out, Sue Ann Pratt had joked before they left. Of course, it also meant girls' night out. That was okay, Ed had figured. She might not be in a joking mood later. Or maybe she would? It was a funny world.

Ed Beasly owned a classic car company located in Kendal. You wouldn't mistake his lot for the Pebble Beach Concourse but occasionally he'd get in something nice. Like the perfectly restored T-Bird he'd picked up from the previous owner's widow for a third of its value. 1957 T-Bird. Highly desirable car. A black beauty with portholes in the detachable hardtop. He'd sold it to a guy in South Beach. Yes sir, turned a considerable profit on that little number. Normally, though, his inventory ran just south of average.

The thing about the T-Bird, though, was that his wife had wanted to keep it for herself. She'd always loved, just absolutely adored, that particular model year. Sex on wheels, she called it.

Wasn't going to happen. South Beach was an important market. Big bucks. Getting a foot in there could make all the difference. Besides, he had an expensive boat to pay off. That Whaler with the three Mercs that'd just rocketed them into town didn't come cheap.

So Joan didn't get her T-Bird but instead was taken out to dinner at the new Chinese restaurant in the mall where he also took the opportunity to lay the trip to Key West on her. And that was fine with her, his being out of town. Until he mentioned that Gary would be coming along for the ride. Looking back now, he could understand why she'd been all smiley face until he lowered that boom.

Gary Pratt was an accountant. He did the taxes for Ed's car business. He wasn't a boater like Ed. Sure, boats were nice toys but he preferred to keep his feet on dry ground. It wasn't like he was afraid of water. He was an okay swimmer. Just boats didn't do anything for him. Still, the idea of a weekend in the Keys wasn't something to turn down.

Ed had discovered the hanky-panky by spying on his wife's phone. He'd come home early one day after spending a long lunch at a strip club and she'd been out back futzing around in the flower garden at their place in Coral Gables. He saw the phone lying on a bedroom table and decided to read her e-mail. Not that he was of a suspicious mind or had any reason to be so. He just thought it would be a funny thing to do. Ed enjoyed a little joke now and then. Privacy never entered his mind. Anyway, he knew her password. 1957TBird. As if, really!

The pictures were the first surprise. Shocking, actually. A couple of cock selfies. Well, there are a lot of creeps out there sending that crap everywhere. He was no prude, but poor Joan. Had to happen to her, didn't it? Must've been devastating. Then he saw who the creep was that had sent it. He got e-mails from him every day.

Yeah, he'd never seen the guy's junk but he sure recognized his address. grapra4cpa. Good ol' Gary Pratt.

And there was more. Love notes. Scheduled secret meetings. Always at a goddamn cheap motel! He'd no sooner finished reading the last juicy message than he heard Joan come in. He put the phone down and pulled off his shirt.

"Hi, honey," he shouted. "I'm upstairs changing. Be down in a sec."

He went into the bathroom and rinsed his face with cold water. What the hell was he going to do? Run downstairs and accuse her? Then what? He needed to think. He put on a fresh shirt.

"What are you doing home so early?" Joan asked, walking into the room.

"Got a line on a '68 Camaro," Ed lied. "Down in Homestead. Ran down to take a look. Not one for us."

A pensive expression fell across his face. He couldn't help it.

"Oh, I'm sorry," she said. "Don't be sad. It's a good thing you found out that the car wasn't any good."

"Yeah, you're right. I shouldn't let it get to me."

~~~

Ed soon picked up on the tells whenever he and his wife were together with Gary and Sue Ann. A glance held too long at Gary. Same with a touch of her hand by him. Exaggerated laughter at his asinine jokes. That was even more unbearable. Well, there was that one story about how blue whales could fart a bubble big enough to hold a horse.

Still, it was getting so he could barely hide his hatred for the guy. Imagine, the four of them sitting at a table telling jokes while this bastard was waxing her transom. He was corroding from the inside out. Going to rot. Then murder whispered in his ear.

~~~

Key West was a hell of a place for killing someone. Water all around. Piers to fall from and drown. Dark streets and even darker alleys. Homeless people wandering about. Drunks. Sidewalks so bad a person could trip, hit his head and, bingo, the job was done for you. So many possibilities and yet he hadn't found the right one. Well, as they say, the night is young.

And this being their first night in town, Ed suggested they bar crawl Duval.

~~~

"Why don't you stick up your business card?" Ed

laughed. "Might get an emergency call."

They were at Captain Tony's, where Hemingway was said to have hung out until that tragic day the owner raised the price of a drink and Ernest walked out and up the street to Sloppy Joe's, vowing never to return. Inside Tony's, every square inch is covered with about a zillion business cards tacked up. Gary inserted one of his own in a bunch on the wall next to the bar.

"How 'bout you, Ed?" Gary shouted above the guitarist who'd just launched into *Margaritaville*. "Might sell another T-Bird."

"No, everybody in here is too drunk to think about driving."

They finished their beers and decided to work their way uptown. The promenade was in full swing by the time they came to the Bull, having made a stop or two along the way. Rock 'n roll blasting out on the sidewalk drew them inside. It was packed and Ed had to shoulder his way up to the bar.

"Let's have a shot," he said to Gary.

Two rums later and Gary was on the dance floor doing the Twist. He wasn't a bad dancer and the girl he'd asked was getting into it.

Look at the bastard, Ed grumbled to himself. Who does he think he is? Ed had struck out with the girl's friend. He ordered another shot. Only one. Gary could get his own damn drink.

"Let's blow this joint," Ed said when Gary returned. "Maybe head back to the boat."

Gary seemed a little disappointed but agreed. They walked back to Greene and over to the Bight.

"How about one more at Turtle Kraals," Ed suggested.

A few customers sat at the bar. Ed and Gary pulled out a couple of stools and plopped down.

"What'll it be, gents?" the bartender asked.

"Two Buds," Ed told him.

"What's the story on this place?" Gary asked when the beers were brought. "What's its name mean?"

"Years ago, turtles used to be kept in the kraals outside there," the man explained. "Kraal is a Dutch word for corral. They'd catch the turtles, store them here before butchering. Big business back then. Turtles are protected now."

"What kind of turtles did they catch?"

"Hell, I don't know. Turtles."

"That's sad."

"Yeah, well, it didn't always go so good for the turtlers either," the bartender grinned. "There's a story about one of them that lost his hand. Had it bitten off. Probably a snapper. I've seen those damn things. Wouldn't want to be skinny-dipping with one of them around, if you know what I mean. Anyway, some nights you can hear that old turtler clumping along the boardwalk looking for his lost hand."

"That's so much bullshit," Ed said.

"Yeah? Lots of people swear they've heard it."

"We're tied up right behind the kraal," Gary said. "We'll listen for him."

"You believe that shit?" Ed said once the bartender had left.

"Strange things happen. You can't explain everything, Ed."

"You know, you're dumber than that asshole. Ready for another?"

~~~

Back on board the Whaler – Ed hadn't decided on a name for it yet – the two of them sat in the cabin having a nightcap. Action had wound down to boring at the Kraal and Ed remembered they had an ice chest full of beer on the boat. Besides, they might be able to snag some babes strolling by with the offer of a cool one from such a cool couple of guys as themselves. Yeah, sure.

Ed fired up a cigar while Gary popped open another can and handed it to him.

"I'm still thinking about that turtler," Gary said. "I read a book about catching turtles down in the Caribbean. Can't remember its title. Great story, though."

Ed took a deep puff, the end of the cigar glowing like a port navigation light.

"Tell you what, Gary. Since we haven't made the sleeping arrangements, why don't you bunk down out here. If that guy comes looking for his lost hand or lost shaker of salt or whatever the hell he's lost, you can help him find it."

Gary laughed and agreed.

"Sure. It's warm. I'll just sink in the chair and be off to lullaby land."

The two men sat back, enjoying their beers and listening to the music drift over from Schooner Wharf.

"Say, Ed, I was wondering about those motors," Gary said with a slight slur and pointing to the stern. "Why so many?"

"Horsepower, my man," Ed answered proudly. "Each one of those babies puts out 300 horses. That's how we got down here quick as a bunny."

"Guess it's a good thing to have three, huh? In case one breaks down."

"The only thing that'd stop them, other than running out of gas, would be to foul the propeller," Ed said. "Rarely happens out on the open water. In the harbor you might run into some shit."

"What would you do then? I mean, to free the propeller?"

"Well, you'd reach down and remove whatever was caught in it."

"That'd be pretty dangerous, wouldn't it?"

"Well, hell yes, if you left it in gear and the propellers were turning – duh."

Ed suddenly realized he'd just stumbled on to one of the fifty ways to kill your wife's lover. He smiled and shook his head in wonderment. Then a bolt of inspiration flashed.

"I know about you and Joan," he said. "You son of a bitch, what the hell were you thinking?"

"Now wait a minute," Gary said nervously. "Take it easy!"

"Don't worry. I'm not going to get crazy. Just wanted you to know that Joan and I talked it out. We're going to see a marriage counselor. But it's over, Gary, between you and Joan. Get that straight in your fucking head!"

"I don't know what to say, Ed. Suppose I should leave, huh? Find a place to stay for the night, catch a plane back home tomorrow."

"Don't be such a dumb fuck," Ed laughed. "Sure, it was a crappy thing you did. Screwing your partner's wife? Pretty low, man. Pretty low."

"I didn't start it," he said. "I mean, it just sort of happened."

"Just one of those things, huh?" Ed laughed sarcastically.

He was enjoying making Gary squirm. Now he had something to hold over the bastard. He was in control. And he was going to relish every delicious moment.

"I know," he continued. "Could've happened to any one of us. Tell you the truth, I've come close myself. Show me any man who says he can look at a woman for five minutes without thinking pussy, huh? No way, Jose. Wired into our head."

Gary smiled sheepishly and nodded.

Ed returned the smile. He had him now, boy, did he ever!

Robert Coburn

"But that doesn't mean you've got to act on it," Ed said. "Sure, look if you want. But keep your pecker in your pants. See? That's your problem. You acted on the situation. Screwed my wife! You disrespected me, man. Put my honor at stake. I don't know."

"I said I'm sorry, man. You're right, I should've just looked and not touched, okay? But it's over. I swear."

"Over, huh? Well, it better fucking be over. Suppose I'd been hitting on Sue Ann? She's a good-looking piece. You like that? Me calling her a piece? Yeah, it's not so funny. And you'd have been pissed, am I right?"

"Yeah, Ed, I would have been pissed. But you know what? It wouldn't have been the first time."

This news gave Ed some pause. What the hell did Gary just say? That his old lady was running around on him? Well, damn!

"Hey, didn't mean to come down so hard," he said. You're right, it was just one of those things. I can understand that. Let's have another pop and then hit the sack. Last day tomorrow."

~~~

Dawn cracked without an ounce of pity for the past night's revelers. The Bight was full awake at first light and going about its business. Fishing boats setting out early for the reefs, the rumble of powerful engines carrying across the water. Gulls clamoring overhead. Some sadistic prick even had a radio blaring.

"You dead or alive?" Ed asked, shaking Gary's shoulder.

"Oh, shit," Gary answered, painfully sitting up in the chair.

"Get your toothbrush and shaving kit," Ed told him. "The public restroom's right up there. Don't have much more than a small head here on the boat."

"About last night, Ed. I'm sorry as all hell."

"Didn't I say it was over? Forget it. What I want to know is, did you hear the ghost? You know, the turtle fisherman looking for his hand?"

"Yeah, he came by and I helped him look but we couldn't find the damn thing," Gary chuckled.

~~~

Breakfast at Turtle Kraals is a treat. No only is the food good but up on the tower they throw in a billion dollar view of some of the biggest yachts in the world at no extra cost.

"Man, I can't imagine what it must be like to be on one of those things," Gary said through a mouthful of scrambled eggs. "How big do you think those two are over there?"

He pointed to two super yachts berthed port to starboard across the harbor.

"Got to be more than a hundred feet long," Ed said. "Maybe even a hundred and fifty. Lot of bucks, man. You're talking millions."

"Yeah, must cost a fortune to run one, too."

"Like the man said, if you got to ask, you can't afford it."

~~~

The tide would be favorable at four that afternoon. Ed told Gary that would give them plenty of time to get back to Miami before dark. They decided to take another stroll along Duval.

Wouldn't you just know it? Right at the Tree Bar next to Rick's sat two lovelies all by themselves. Ed slid onto a barstool next to one. She was the blonde and a knockout. The other was brunette, and as Ed liked to say, nothing you'd kick out of bed. The girls had just gotten to town and were ready to party down.

"It's a great day for drinking," Ed said, leaning over to the girl. He'd picked up the line from a bartender at the little Tiki.

"What's the best bar in Key West?" she asked.

"Depends on what you're looking for," Ed answered coolly and with a leer.

"Some place fun," she said.

"Then you should try the Whaler."

"Where is it?"

"My boat."

"You have a boat? Oh, my goodness! Is it big?"

"Big enough for the four of us to party on," Ed grinned. "Want to see it?"

"Thought we had to leave by four," Gary whispered to Ed.

"So we'll make it five," Ed said. "Plenty of time."

Right then one of the girls, the blonde whose name incredibly happened to be Joan, shrieked.

"John! William!" And then to her girlfriend, "OhmyGod, look who's here, Nance! It's John and William from the ferry!"

Nance, the brunette who wouldn't have been kicked out of bed, squealed and jiggled on her seat.

John and William sauntered over from the sidewalk. Both girls greeted them with big hugs.

"Wow, I didn't think we'd see you guys again so soon," Joan gushed. "Oh, by the way, this is Ed and Gary. They have a boat. We were just going there."

"Hey, that's great," the new arrivals said, almost in unison. "Okay if we tag along?"

The girls squealed.

Ed picked his face from off the floor where it'd fallen and looked at his watch.

"Oh, damn, I'm sorry, guys," he said. "We have to split for Miami. Time and tide wait for no man, ha-ha."

~~~

On the way back to the Bight, they stopped at

Schooner Wharf. There was a good crowd and the music was pleasant. Schooner is an inside-outside kind of place with a large bar inside, tables scattered around on the outside grounds in front of the stage, and thought of by all as a landmark institution.

Ed ordered two rums and coke.

"Here's to nothing," he said to Gary, lifting his drink and casting an eye around.

"You know, you're a hypocrite," Gary laughed.

"What?"

"You know what. All that crap about being disrespected. When back at that last bar you were busting your ass trying to pick up those two girls. And just now, checking out this bar. Man, you don't give up, do you?"

"You getting all holy Joe on me, pal?" Ed said angrily.

"No, I'm just saying before you go knocking me, take a good look at yourself. You ready for another drink?"

Gary motioned to the bartender. Two rums and coke were quickly set in front of them.

"Cheers," Gary said.

"It was my wife you were banging!" Ed said loudly. "Don't forget that!"

A couple of people looked over. One man at the end of the bar gave a little chuckle. Ed glared at him and the man turned his head away.

"That's right, Ed," Gary said calmly. "But if you're so concerned about the sanctity of marriage, what the hell have you been doing since we got here? I know you fuck around. So give it a break."

'You don't know jack shit, Gary. Drink up and let's get the hell out of here."

~~~

The walk to the boat's mooring went without incident. Ed nodding to passersby and Gary taking note of the larger yachts. Ed stepped aboard.

"I'm going to check out the engines," he said. "You stay up here to handle the lines. I'll tell you when to untie us."

That was fine with Gary. He really wasn't all that excited to start back to Miami. It had even crossed his mind after they'd left the Schooner to tell Ed to leave without him. He wouldn't mind another night on his own in Key West. And Sue Ann sure as hell wouldn't care.

Ed ran the checks. It was time to go. He started the engines.

The 300 hp Mercs fired quickly and in order. One. Two. Three. Now all three were quietly purring like big cats. Ed standing at the wheel.

"Loose the aft lines, Gary," he shouted. "Then the bow."

Gary untied the lines and came aboard himself.

Ed eased the Whaler out of its berth and began a slow trip to the end of the breakwater.

"You're full of shit," Gary said, coming up to Ed.

"What now?"

"That thing you said about you and Joan? She told you about us? Never happened. And you two are going to a marriage counselor? That's laughable, Ed."

Ed put the motors into neutral.

"It's true, you dickhead," he said.

"No, it's a lie. Like everything else about you. Joan knew you'd looked at her email. She told me. So all that crap is just that. Crap!"

This wasn't good, Ed thought. He was supposed to be the one in control. What was this jerk up to? He put the motors back in gear.

"You should've given her the T-Bird," Gary continued.

"That's none of your business," Ed snapped.

"Oh, but it is," Gary countered. "You see, Ed, I do your taxes. You can't hide the profit like you've been doing. You really needed a write-off. This little toy we're on now isn't going to fly, as far as the Feds are concerned. You're screwed, old boy. Big-time."

They were coming to the mouth of the harbor. It was now or never. He'd planned for this moment. Thought he had everything worked out. Sweetened it with his reverse psychology in telling Gary he knew about the affair. Then Gary seemed to have outplayed him. Took control again. Well, he'd see about that! Ed shut down one engine.

"Damn it, Gary. Didn't I tell you to keep an eye out for trash? Now we've fouled a propeller."

He put the other two engines in neutral and walked to the stern. The Whaler bobbed happily, the tide at the high mark and just beginning to turn. The sun hovered above the horizon to the west.

"Looks like a plastic bag or something," he said, reaching down to the motor's lower unit. "Hell, I can't get it. Gary, come here and see if those long arms of yours can free this thing."

"You didn't say anything about keeping an eye out, Ed."

"Well, it's too damn late now," Ed said. "Take a look at this mess."

Gary bent down to see what he was talking about. Ed stood up and grabbed his shoulders from the back, and, with a push, sent him sprawling over the transom.

But Gary managed to get ahold of the engine control cable to keep from falling into the water. He got his legs under him. Ed was on him then with his fists.

The two men struggled and fell to the deck.

~~~

A hundred yards away from the Whaler, the super yacht *So Nice* entered the harbor from the Bight making five knots. The sun reflected brightly off its massive windshields.

The Whaler's engines had engaged themselves when Gary

had grabbed the control cable and now was about cross the yacht's path directly in front. The captain saw the impending danger too late to change course. The 164-footer crunched into the Whaler broadside, rolling the smaller boat under its bow.

~~~

Wreckage floated in a wide area. Divers found the two men, oddly enough, in the forward compartment, the only intact piece left of the boat. They surmised that the twisting and turbulence after the impact had forced them into the space. Also, the yacht's twin screws had contributed to the further destruction. The recovered bodies mirrored the results.

The authorities suspected alcohol to have been involved. A later autopsy confirmed that. The *So Nice* was towed to a shipyard in Miami for repairs. Two months later she sailed for the Mediterranean Sea and Italy.

~~~

Agnes Brown and her son, Justin, were watching a pair of small tarpon in the pool at the Turtle Kraal. Her husband, Jim, was away at the moment, looking into getting tickets for a sunset cruise. This was the Browns' first trip to Key West. Justin pointed to something in the shallow water. A funny fish, he said to his mom. Agnes squinted to get a better look. Then she gasped and pulled Justin back from the rail.

~~~

The police dip-netted the human hand from the water. It had apparently been in there for some time. Probably a crab had carried it into the pool, one of the cops had speculated. The hand was sent to Miami for DNA testing and later proved to be Ed Beasley's.

~~~

No one has since heard the old turtler clomping along the boardwalk at night.

10.
M FOR MURDER

Barthélemy Banks

Malloy had been falling-down-drunk in Key West for a good ten years before he got the call from his old handler. "Jeez, B, how did you find me?"

In his section of the CIA they used letters of the alphabet as cryptonyms. It worked. With the agency's compartmentalization, he doubted he knew 26 people in total. He could count them on his fingers: His primary contact, the mysterious officer known as B; his partner; a few on-the-job operatives; not many more. He supposed the Director was known as A, but no one had ever told him. Need to know and all that.

"We keep tabs," said B. His voice sounded distant over the phone. Not that Malloy – or M as he was called by his old agency contacts – even had a mobile phone. He'd long ago traded his iPhone for a drink.

But here he sat in the Hog's Breath Saloon, elbows on the bar, nursing a whiskey sour, when the guy next to him turned and handed him a phone, saying "This call's for you."

B, out of the blue.

"What can I do for you?" Malloy grunted. "You having a reunion of the old ZRIFLE gang?" That was the team of assassins Malloy had worked with when he'd been an officer in good standing. Before all the booze.

"Just you. A reunion of one, you might call it. Need

you to look into something down there in the Conch Republic." That was a fanciful name for Key West, the result of an early '80s protest against tight drug enforcement in a smugglers' town. The island ceremonially seceded from the union, then immediately surrendered and demanded a billion dollars in war reparations as a way of embarrassing the DEA into lifting its stop-and-search roadblocks. It worked. The roadblocks came down, but the war reparations were never paid. And the name stuck, at least on flags and T-shirts.

"I've been out of the game too long," Malloy protested. "My hands shake. Or haven't you heard about my search for a lost shaker of salt?"

"We heard. But you're the man for the job."

"What job?"

"A square grouper washed up at Smathers Beach this morning."

"A bale of marijuana?"

"Yeah, but this one had a body in it. We need you to identify it."

Malloy snorted. "Why not send the guy who handed me this phone? I assume he's one of your boys."

"He wouldn't be able to ID the body. We think it's J."

"J – my old team mate?"

The voice on the phone sounded sad. "One and the same. Bernie Jackson. But let's hope we're wrong. Let's hope you say you've never seen this dead guy before in your whole life."

"Jeez," Malloy repeated. He had been a shooter; J had been his spotter. Same principle as with snipers, but Malloy – or M as he'd been known – was an up-and-close specialist, using a .22 pistol to put a hollow point into an enemy target's brain. The soft spot behind the ear was usually the most effective way to do the job. He'd racked up over two-dozen confirmed kills, more than most serial killers.

"The body's still at Smathers Beach. The police have cordoned it off. They are waiting for you to take a look-see."

"How do I get there? Somebody stole my bicycle." Truth is, he'd traded it for a pint of Jack Daniels.

"T will take you. He's got a car."

"T?"

"The guy who lent you the phone."

"Oh."

"So you'll do it?"

"Yeah, for J – not for you."

~ ~ ~

Malloy and the man known as T drove to Smathers Beach. Over the Palm Avenue Bridge and straight out 1st Street to Bertha. A scenic route if you consider Garrison Bight with all its charter boats and floating houseboats and ritzy yacht club.

The police were holding back a small crowd of onlookers. They parted like the Red Sea to let Malloy and T pass. The square grouper that had washed up on the sand was a polyethylene-wrapped rectangle about the size of a bale of hay. It had broken open and a man's head and torso were exposed to the morning sun.

The bright light hurt Malloy's eyes. Even at this time of the morning he was usually sitting in a shadowy bar. Sometimes he drank at Don's Million Dollar Bar, letting it close down at 4 a.m. according to law, while its patrons continued drinking in the dark until it officially opened again at 7.

"Recognize him?" asked a burly policeman.

Malloy peered down at the body. Fairly fresh, not bloated yet. He bent to examine the head. A tiny hole behind the ear, a professional hit. The small-caliber dum-dum had rattled around inside the cranium like beads inside a gourd, a killing shot. Not a good sign, this method of execution. CIA shooters and Israeli Mossed used .22s. The mob preferred cannons like a .45 and Colombian drug lords liked FN-57 pistols, or AR 223 and AK 7.62 rifles.

Nothing here for the Mossed. Did that mean this was an official Company sanction? No – if it were, B never would have called him to verify the hit.

The dead man was Bernie Jackson, not doubt about it. Same mole on his right cheek. Same bushy eyebrows. But his eyes looked different, staring blankly, as if catching a glimpse of the after life.

Malloy turned to the man called T. "That's our boy."

"Yeah, I recognize the mole."

They stepped away from the body to talk. It was important to get their stories straight before giving the police J's name. Malloy glanced at the crowd but didn't recognize any faces. "Who else is down here?"

"In Key West. A handful of us. There's an office here you know."

"No, I mean covert types. Like you and me."

"How would I know? Covert is covert. But it's not like the old days."

By the "old days" he meant the '60s during the Cuban Missile Crisis. Back then the island was crawling with CIA men. Rocket launchers lining the beaches. Electronic listening posts inside the entrance to the Naval Base. Missile silos out near the airport, humps of sand with tunnels underneath. Black boats leaving Stock Island under the dark of night. Custom agents on the CIA payroll. Gerry Hemming training those Interpen paramilitaries on No Name Key. William Harvey King planning murders with Johnny Roselli on a boat off Islamorada. Alpha 66 and Bay of Pigs survivors and spies of all persuasions.

No, it wasn't like the old days.

"What was J working on?"

"How would I know? I'm just a flunky. I take orders, don't give 'em."

Despite blurry eyes and throbbing head, Malloy paused to study his companion. A sharp dresser, the $2,000 suit indicating expensive taste for a lowly field agent. Lots of bling, a stud earring, a diamond pinkie ring the size of an aggie marble. There was a disconnect here somewhere.

"How long you been stationed here?"

T shrugged. "Six or seven years."

"Funny we've never met."

"No need to. Till now."

"But it's a small island. Eight square miles."

T smirked. "I've seen you around, Malloy. Usually smashed out of your skull. You really fell off the charts. They don't even have me make reports on you anymore."

"I decided I'd rather drink than kill people."

"Not a good career decision for a shooter." T studied his fingernails – manicured judging from the perfect cuticles.

"Guess not. But it was me they called for this job."

T frowned. "That's because you could identify J."

"You knew him too."

"What makes you think that?"

Malloy shrugged. "You recognized the mole."

"Oh that. So I knew him. Big deal."

Malloy toed the sand, thinking about his next words. "Last time I talked with J, he told me he had moved from the Company to the DEA. Special assignment or some such."

"When was that?" T looked uneasy, as if ready to leave the beach, head back to Duval Street.

"A few months ago."

"So he became a narc. What's that got to do with the price of beans?"

Malloy studied the man for a moment, then cut to the chase. "Tell me, T – how long you been in the drug trade?"

"Are you fucking crazy. I'm CIA just like you. Well, like you used to be."

"Maybe so, but those are pretty fancy duds for your pay grade. Gotta be raking in some gravy on the side. Either you've sold out to the Cubans or the Ruskies. Or to one of the Colombian cartels."

"Haven't you heard? Obama's lifting sanctions on the Cubans. Fidel and his brother aren't enemies anymore. And the Russians have troubles of their own – their economy, the Ukraine. They don't give a rat's ass about Cuba these days."

"That leaves drugs. And J did wash up in a bale of maryjane."

T rolled his eyes. "Nobody has called it that since the '70s."

"What do you call it – ganja? Or simply a payload?"

"You can't prove anything, you washed-up old drunk. Find your own way back to Hog's Breath or the Smokin' Tuna. I'm leaving."

"Before you go, let me see your weapon. I bet it's a .22 – right?"

T faced off against Malloy. "Why don't you try taking it, old man? I'll shove it up your ass and pull the trigger."

"Standard Company weaponry is 9mm. Only shooters use a 22-caliber."

T offered him an icy smile. "I used to be a shooter. Before I got assigned here. So sure, I still prefer a .22 when it comes to wet work."

"You must have really fucked up to get busted from being a shooter to a second-rate field man."

"That's none of your affair. But I've done well for myself here in Key West. File a few meaningless reports to Langley, then clear the way for a few shipments from

Mexico. Where do you get this Colombian shit?"

"You killed J. That was a small-caliber hole behind his ear. Besides you and me, I doubt there are any other CIA shooters on the island."

"What do you care? Everybody knows you left the Company because your wife left you for Jackson. That's why you became a lush."

"But I didn't kill him. You did."

"Nobody's going to believe you. You're just a confused alkie. B's not going to take your word against mine."

"We'll see about that." Malloy made as if to turn his back on the dapper man, but continued turning, spinning in an arc, gathering kinetic energy, throwing a hard right hook to T's chin. The man's head snapped back, his body following. He landed with a *thud!* on the powdery white sand.

"What's going on?" shouted the burly policeman. Suddenly Malloy and the downed man were surrounded by a phalanx of cops.

"Careful," Malloy cautioned. "The guy's carrying a gun. A .22, probably holstered in the small of his back."

"A gun? Just who the hell are you two? The Chief said you guys had juice from Washington, but damned if I'm gonna have any brawls at my crime scene."

"You can close the books on this one. The dead man was working with the DEA. This character on the ground is in league with Mexican drug smugglers. He pulled the trigger."

"You can prove this?"

One of the other cops cut him off. "This .22 Beretta's been fired recently," he held up the semi-automatic pistol. "And the clip's short one round."

"Do the ballistics," suggested Malloy. "Then you'll have your proof."

T – it turns out his name was Harley Thompson – sat

up, rubbing his chin. "Doesn't matter. You can't hold me. Langley will spring me."

"Maybe," allowed Tim Malloy. "But they don't let rogue elephants run around shooting people. A colleague will call on you. The Company cleans up its own messes."

The truth of his words was reflected in T's eyes. "Wait, Malloy, maybe you can speak to B, put in a word for me. I can cut you in. I've got plenty of money."

"Forget it. You killed my old partner. And like Sam Spade said, 'When a man's partner is killed, he's supposed to do something about it. It doesn't make any difference what you thought of him. He was your partner and you're supposed to do something about it.'" He flipped Harley Thompson the bird. "Consider this my doing something about it."

He turned to the burly cop. "Say, could one of your men give me a lift to Hog's Breath. I didn't get to finish my whiskey sour."

THE WRITER'S END
a KEY WEST STORY
BY JONATHAN WOODS
ILLUSTRATED BY DAHLIA WOODS

11.
THE WRITER'S END

Jonathan Woods

Sitting on the porch of a white frame house dating from the 19th Century in Old Town Key West, the writer writes. He wears white cotton shorts, his pale linen shirt unbuttoned. With one hand he accidentally brushes back his thinning apricot-colored hair.

The early Sunday morning light of a tropical autumn is as soft and breathless as a blond bimbo. Palm fronds snicker in a slight, salubrious breeze. The sun glints off an empty bourbon bottle abandoned on the street corner by some derelict of the night.

The writer drinks with care. No rip-roaring bouts of drunken mayhem. No hooch inspired Hell-bound hallucinations or whimpered boozy confessions.

The writer is a professional; the scribbler of a dozen film scripts credited and un-credited. In his youth a book of poems, now forgotten. And most recently the let-it-all-hang-out Hollywood memoir that has made him famous and infamous. There is no one more hated or feared in Hollywood. He is the agent provocateur of gossip, tittle-tattle, innuendo and snitchery. Wherever he goes, children point him out in the street. No one will tell him their life story.

The writer attends a grand party held in a grand Key West home overlooking the tennis courts and winos in the park across from Higgs Beach. *Everyone* is there. The ex-senator, the ex-senator's wife, the ex-senator's mistress, businessmen dripping with wealth, their wives dripping with diamonds, lesser literati, producers, actors, musicians & camp followers. The crème de la crème of Conch society.

A tall, lanky blonde wearing very little very well, whose husband is worth a billion or so, mostly offshore, touches the writer's arm:

"What are you working on now, darling?"

The writer, looking demure as a tomcat who moments before swallowed a foie gras-fed mouse, sips his Perrier Jouet and smiles as thinly as a lemon slice.

"I never talk about my work in progress," he says.

Later someone whispers to someone else: After the party he saw the writer sitting in the park feverishly scribbling in his Moleskine, oblivious to the snarling and bickering drunks at the next bench. Making notes of the sidelong glances, the hushed offers of infidelity, the deep cleavages, fat wallets and stolen kisses amid the party throng.

Like frenzied gulls feeding on chum, the rumors fly through the narrow tropical streets of old Key West. The writer is writing a tell-all memoir of his time in the Conch Republic. He is penning a searing roman à clef filled with Key West's glitterati. Vanity Fair to paying him a princely sum for an expose of Key West's demimonde. He has a vendetta against the southernmost island town because of

Murder in Key West 2

a spring break incident lost in the foggy past of his years at Yale.

The writer engages in a bedroom romp with a famously bodacious redheaded starlet. They make the bedsprings squeak like an old Chevy on a dirt road to paradise. With homes in San Moritz, the Hamptons, Malibu and St. Barts, she's slumming in Key West. One moment she's naked except for a pair of fiery red undies. Next moment she's just naked. When she cums, she bellows like a water buffalo.

Afterward, while the writer takes a piss, she flicks

through the papers on his desk, rifles amidst his underwear and shirts in the chest of drawers, breaks a fingernail trying to pick the lock of his portable file cabinet. In vain she tries a dozen passwords to gain entrance to the writer's laptop. Access denied. The only damning evidence she finds is a list of names of some fat cat locals, part-time celebrity residents and high-flying hookers. She's #8 on the list.

A famous gay playwright offers the writer a blowjob and a gram of excellent coke for the torrid details of the writer's new book. The writer blows him off. The playwright leaves the upscale Duval Street restaurant in a huff. Depressed, he goes on a weekend bender of crank, booze, barbiturates and unsafe sex.

Accidentally on purpose the wife of the ex-senator runs into the writer at a French creperie on Petronius. It's eight in the morning and she's already three sheets to the wind. The writer is having breakfast.

"Your last book gave me chills," she says, as she empties her entire gunmetal flask of Jack Daniel's into the writer's café au lait. "I hope your new one will get me off."

The writer suddenly remembers he has an appointment elsewhere, downs his coffee in two quick swallows, rolls his eyes at the amount of liquor he has just consumed and staggers to the door. "We'll get together again soon," he says.

"You bet," she says.

After midnight the writer rides his bicycle back from listening to a reggae band at the Green Parrot.

A deputy sheriff related by marriage to the former senator stops the writer near the old cemetery in the middle of the island. The deputy tells the writer his red taillight is out.

Murder in Key West 2

"That's bullshit!" says the inebriated writer, pointing at the flashing red light on the rear fender of his bike.

"You smell like a fucking liquor store," the deputy says, "I could throw you in the drunk tank, confiscate your wheels."

"Whatever," the writer says.

Without warning the deputy spins the writer around and scoops one arm across his neck, pats down his pockets. When the deputy releases the writer, he holds a baggie of dark green herb.

"This is a fucking set up!" vents the writer. "I don't smoke pot. It makes me jittery."

"The senator doesn't like you," the deputy says. "Doesn't like you having breakfast with his wife. If I were you, I'd move up the coast to Boca Raton before the shit hits the fan." The deputy opens the baggie and turns it upside down. The night wind catches the oregano, scattering it hither and yon.

Despite endless invitations to all manner of garden parties, fetes, theater after parties, grand balls and literary salons among Key West's cognoscenti, the writer is feeling nervous. As though the wolves are closing in. That he is friendless. A failure at love. Being followed by Albanian thugs. Constipated with writer's block. Unable to get it up since the starlet episode.

He suffers night sweats, inexplicable bouts of diarrhea. He senses fear and anger in the eyes of everyone he meets.

His agent keeps calling from New York, asking to see a draft of the new book. "Just send me whatever the fuck you want to share with me!" he yells at the writer. "But send me something!"

The writer calls Bob in L.A. Bob is his oldest friend. When the memoir came out Bob threw a fit and threatened to kill the writer. The writer has a short memory.

On the phone the writer confesses his paranoia, that he's having a little problem with sex. That he's on the verge of a crackup.

"You're dead meat in L.A.," warns Bob. "You're smart just to lay low in the Keys."

"Come for a visit," pleads the writer. "My cigar roller's house has two bedrooms."

Bob catches the next flight from L.A. He checks his bag containing an antique stiletto stashed between his shirts.

The writer is invited to a pig roast on the beach. Dark rum flows from a Blackbeardian oak cask. The most beautiful women of Key West dance on the beach in risqué outfits. Some go naked; paint themselves with voodoo art.

At the pig roast the writer is drinking Cachaca with lime juice and sugar and telling L.A. stories. A woman with nifty tits pulls him away to dance on the sand.

The writer sways drunkenly. Suddenly everyone dancing is wearing carnival masks. Everyone is anonymous.

The writer's dance partner swings him in a circle by one arm. When he spins free and falls backward onto the sand, the knives come out.

The dying writer, wallowing in a pool of his own blood, sighs and looks up at the snarling, circling wolves. Two of the figures remove their masks. One is the ex-senator. The other is Bob.

"Et tu, Bob?" whispers the writer as Bob's stiletto slides into his flesh as easy as a hot knife through butter.

❈ ❈ ❈

About The Authors

1.

Vampire Slayer Murdered in Key West
By Michael Haskins

Michael Haskins says, "I grew up in North Quincy, Massachusetts, and went through the public school system. I wasn't a student who stood out. If my English teacher in the ninth grade had not told me to put down a copy of Hemingway's short stories (I had taken it off a bookrack during study class) because I was 'too stupid to understand it,' I might never have wanted to read. Thank you Mr. Carlin! In my senior year, I talked my creative writing teacher, Mrs. Shapiro, into getting the school to allow us to publish a creative writing magazine, Counterpoint. Mr. Carlin barely passed me, Mrs. Shapiro gave me A's! Go figure!"

"Vampire Slayer Murdered in Key West" was nominated for a Shamus Award.

2.
The Mystery of Marina Merrick
By Heather Graham

New York Times and USA Today best selling author, Heather Graham is the child of Scottish and Irish immigrants who met and married in Chicago, and moved to South Florida, where she has spent her life. She majored in theater arts at the University of South Florida. After a stint of several years in dinner theater, back-up vocals, and bartending, she stayed home after the birth of her third child and began to write. Her first book was with Dell, and since then, she has written over one hundred and fifty novels and novellas.

3.
Last Chance
By Bill Craig

Bill Craig taught himself to read at age four and began writing his own stories at age six. He published his first novel at age 40 and says it only took him 34 years to become an overnight success! He has been publishing steadily ever since that first book *Valley of Death* and now has 27 books in print or ebook. This is the second entry in his bestselling Marlow series.

4.
Disturbance in the Field
By Roberta Isleib
Writing as Lucy Burdette

Lucy Burdette A/K/A Roberta Isleib is a clinical psychologist and the author of ten mysteries, including the Key West food critic series. Her books and stories have been short-listed for Agatha, Anthony, and Macavity awards. She is a past president of Sisters in Crime.

5.
The Walls Had Ears: Murder at 2929
By Ben Harrison

Ben Harrison was born in San Antonio, Texas, and spent his early years in Corpus Christi. Earning an undergraduate degree at Southern Methodist, he graduated from their law school in 1972. He and his wife Helen moved to San Francisco, then drove to Costa Rica where they built the 31-foot sailboat they lived on for 11 years. In 1979 they sailed to Key West, Florida, where he became a professional musician, songwriter, and author. In 1982 they opened Harrison Gallery.

6.
Better Times Than These
By William R. Burkett, Jr.

William R. Burkett, Jr. is better known as a science fiction writer, but this foray into the mean streets of the world of Dashiell Hammett and Ross MacDonald and Raymond Chandler is formidable – tough, engaging, and as jarring as a nail scraped across a blackboard. *Twin Killing* was the initial book in his Rainy City Mystery series, followed by *Family Skeleton*. Here his hard-as-nails Seattle sleuth visits Key West.

7.
The Impresario
By Hal Howland

Hal Howland is the author of *After Jerusalem: A Story and Two Novellas*, *The Human Drummer: Thoughts on the Life Percussive,* and *Landini Cadence and Other Stories: A Rich Castillo Threesome,* a finalist in the 2011 Next Generation Indie Book Awards and a recipient of the 2012 Eric Hoffer Award for excellence in independent publishing. Several pieces in *The Jazz Buyer* have been nominated for the Lorian Hemingway Short Story Competition and the *Writer's Digest* Popular Fiction Awards. Howland has released three award-winning, critically acclaimed jazz recordings, *The Howland Ensemble, Reiko,* and *10 Years in 5 Days,* and has received a jazz fellowship from the National Endowment for the Arts. Born in Washington, D.C., and raised in Virginia, Europe, and the Middle East, Howland lives in Key West, Florida.

8.

Four Fingers and the Acerbic Film Critic
By Shirrel Rhoades

Shirrel Rhoades is a writer, critic, filmmaker, former college professor, art collector, museum president, and publishing consultant. These days, he calls Key West home. He is the author of *Four Fingers Four Minute Mysteries. The Devil's Hop Yard,* and *Front Row at the Movies,* among other titles. He and his wife share their historic classic temple revival style house in Old Town with a dog and 1 ½ cats and sometimes even a pretty TV morning show host. But that's another story.

9.
Hand-Fed Snapping Turtles
By Robert Coburn

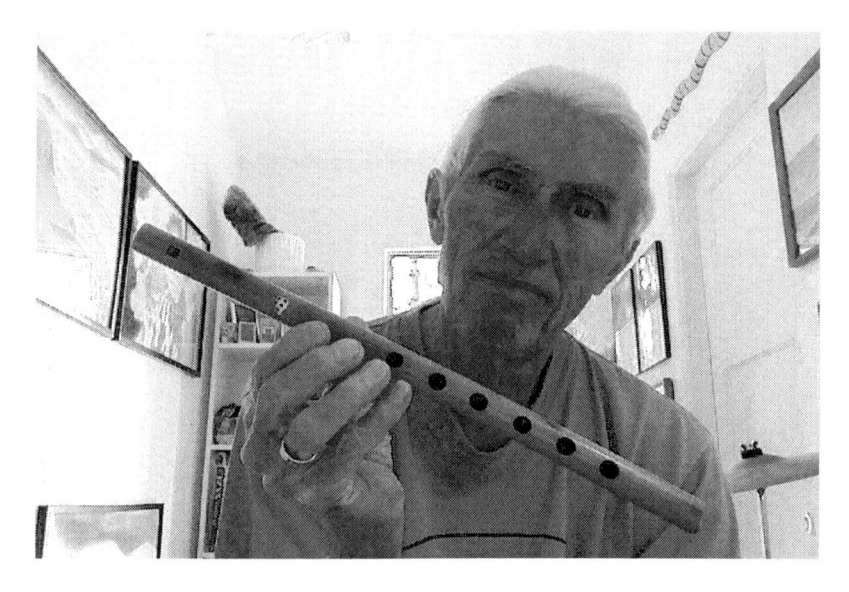

Robert Coburn is originally from Norfolk, Virginia. After high school in Norfolk, he spent three years in the US Army as a helicopter crew chief stationed in Berlin, Germany. He returned home to attend college at Richmond Professional Institute (Now VCU) in Richmond, Virginia, where he earned a Bachelor of Science degree in Advertising. He also met his wife in Richmond while a student there.

Coburn has worked at major advertising agencies in New York and Los Angeles. His ads have won top awards both nationally and internationally. He is an instrument rated commercial pilot and plays saxophone. He and his wife now live in Carmel, California.

10.
M For Murder
By Barthélemy Banks

Barthélemy Banks is the *nom de plume* of a former supervisor for a publishing company that was secretly backed by the CIA. He spent a number of years in the Bahamas where he rubbed elbows with spies, smugglers, international bankers, and reclusive millionaires. Today, he lives on a remote island, where he finds it safe to write about the clandestine world he knows so well.

11.
The Writer's End
By Jonathan Woods

Jonathan Woods holds degrees from McGill University, New England School of Law, and New York University School of Law, and for many years practiced law for a multi-national high-tech company. Jonathan's crime story collection *Bad Juju & Other Tales of Madness and Mayhem* was featured at the 2010 Texas Book Festival and won a 2011 Spinetingler Award for Best Crime Short Story Collection. His short story collection *Phone Call from Hell & Other Tales of the Damned* was published recently. A film based on his story *Swingers Anonymous* was shown at the 2015 Cannes international Film Festival.

ABSOLUTELY AMAZING eBOOKS

AbsolutelyAmazingEbooks.com
or AA-eBooks.com

Made in the USA
Middletown, DE
25 January 2018